# Endangered Species

# OTHER BOOKS OF RELATED INTEREST

# Endangered Species

Shasta Gaughen, *Book Editor*

Bruce Glassman, *Vice President*
Bonnie Szumski, *Publisher*
Helen Cothran, *Managing Editor*
David M. Haugen, *Series Editor*

## Contemporary Issues
### Companion

**GREENHAVEN PRESS**
*An imprint of Thomson Gale, a part of The Thomson Corporation*

THOMSON
GALE

Detroit • New York • San Francisco • San Diego • New Haven, Conn.
Waterville, Maine • London • Munich

*For more information, contact*
Greenhaven Press
27500 Drake Rd.
Farmington Hills, MI 48331-3535
Or you can visit our Internet site at http://www.gale.com

**LIBRARY OF CONGRESS CATALOGING-IN-PUBLICATION DATA**

Endangered species / Shasta Gaughen, book editor.
   p. cm. — (Contemporary issues companion)
  Includes bibliographical references and index.
  ISBN 0-7377-2454-4 (lib. : alk. paper) — ISBN 0-7377-2455-2 (pbk. : alk. paper)
   1. Endangered species. 2. Nature conservation. I. Gaughen, Shasta. II. Series.
QH75.E652 2006
333.95'22—dc22
                                       2005046166

Printed in the United States of America

# CONTENTS

# FOREWORD

In the news, on the streets, and in neighborhoods, individuals are confronted with a variety of social problems. Such problems may affect people directly: A young woman may struggle with depression, suspect a friend of having bulimia, or watch a loved one battle cancer. And even the issues that do not directly affect her private life—such as religious cults, domestic violence, or legalized gambling—still impact the larger society in which she lives. Discovering and analyzing the complexities of issues that encompass communal and societal realms as well as the world of personal experience is a valuable educational goal in the modern world.

Effectively addressing social problems requires familiarity with a constantly changing stream of data. Becoming well informed about today's controversies is an intricate process that often involves reading myriad primary and secondary sources, analyzing political debates, weighing various experts' opinions—even listening to firsthand accounts of those directly affected by the issue. For students and general observers, this can be a daunting task because of the sheer volume of information available in books, periodicals, on the evening news, and on the Internet. Researching the consequences of legalized gambling, for example, might entail sifting through congressional testimony on gambling's societal effects, examining private studies on Indian gaming, perusing numerous websites devoted to Internet betting, and reading essays written by lottery winners as well as interviews with recovering compulsive gamblers. Obtaining valuable information can be time-consuming—since it often requires researchers to pore over numerous documents and commentaries before discovering a source relevant to their particular investigation.

Greenhaven's Contemporary Issues Companion series seeks to assist this process of research by providing readers with useful and pertinent information about today's complex issues. Each volume in this anthology series focuses on a topic of current interest, presenting informative and thought-provoking selections written from a wide variety of viewpoints. The readings selected by the editors include such diverse sources as personal accounts and case studies, pertinent factual and statistical articles, and relevant commentaries and overviews. This diversity of sources and views, found in every Contemporary Issues Companion, offers readers a broad perspective in one convenient volume.

In addition, each title in the Contemporary Issues Companion series is designed especially for young adults. The selections included in every volume are chosen for their accessibility and are expertly edited in consideration of both the reading and comprehension levels of the audience. The structure of the anthologies also enhances accessibility. An introductory essay places each issue in context and provides helpful facts such as historical background or current statistics and legislation that pertain to the topic. The chapters that follow organize the material and focus on specific aspects of the book's topic. Every essay is introduced by a brief summary of its main points and biographical information about the author. These summaries aid in comprehension and can also serve to direct readers to material of immediate interest and need. Finally, a comprehensive index allows readers to efficiently scan and locate content.

The Contemporary Issues Companion series is an ideal launching point for research on a particular topic. Each anthology in the series is composed of readings taken from an extensive gamut of resources, including periodicals, newspapers, books, government documents, the publications of private and public organizations, and Internet websites. In these volumes, readers will find factual support suitable for use in reports, debates, speeches, and research papers. The anthologies also facilitate further research, featuring a book and periodical bibliography and a list of organizations to contact for additional information.

A perfect resource for both students and the general reader, Greenhaven's Contemporary Issues Companion series is sure to be a valued source of current, readable information on social problems that interest young adults. It is the editors' hope that readers will find the Contemporary Issues Companion series useful as a starting point to formulate their own opinions about and answers to the complex issues of the present day.

# INTRODUCTION

Half a billion years ago, at the end of the late Cambrian period of geo-logic history, Earth experienced the first known mass extinction of plant and animal life. Although scientists do not know exactly what caused this extinction, most experts believe that a change in sea level dramatically altered the habitats in which many plants and animals lived, causing them to die out. About 60 million years later, at the end of the late Ordovician period, an ice age caused another massive ex-tinction, with some groups of organisms losing up to half of their species. The end of the Devonian period, approximately 365 million years ago, witnessed yet another series of extinctions. Scientists esti-mate that over a period of five hundred thousand to 3 million years, this extinction event resulted in the loss of up to 70 percent of the planet's species. Researchers have suggested that the Devonian extinc-tions were caused by a period of climate change that resulted in cooler global temperatures.

The Carboniferous and Permian periods, from 360 to 286 million years ago, respectively, saw an explosion in the number of plant and animal species. For more than 100 million years, species diversified and flourished on land and in the sea. The end of the Permian, how-ever, was witness to the single largest extinction event in the history of the planet. Up to 96 percent of all ocean species perished, while up to three-quarters of vertebrates on land disappeared. Scientists believe that the Permian extinction was caused by several factors, including changes in sea level and salinity, volcanic activity, and climate change.

Following this devastating event, the organisms that survived adapted and spread throughout new habitats. During the Cretaceous period, amphibians, dinosaurs and other reptiles, birds, mammals, and flowering plants appeared and multiplied. At the end of the Cre-taceous, 65 million years ago, the most well known extinction event occurred. The Cretaceous extinction saw the loss of 85 percent of the planet's species, including all of the dinosaurs. Scientists believe that this event was most likely caused by a large meteorite striking Earth and causing massive disruptions in the planet's ecosystems.

Today, Earth may be in the middle of the greatest extinction crisis in history. According to the International Union for Conservation of Nature and Natural Resources (IUCN), which publishes the annual *Red List of Threatened Species*, a total of 15,589 plant and animal species faced extinction as of 2004. The IUCN states on its Web site that "one in three amphibians and almost half of all freshwater turtles are threatened, on top of the one in eight birds and one in four mam-mals known to be in jeopardy."

What is causing the rapid rate of species endangerment and potential extinction? Researchers believe that the accelerated decline of species diversity today is due to some of the same factors that caused earlier extinctions, such as climate change and natural alterations in habitat as well as competition among species. However, these researchers also point to a cause that did not play any role in ancient extinctions: human activity. According to two-time Pulitzer Prize–winning Harvard biologist Edward O. Wilson, the spread of humans all over the globe approximately one hundred thousand years ago triggered a massive increase in the rate of species endangerment and extinction. In his 2002 book *The Future of Life* Wilson asserts that before human beings, with their "improved tools, dense populations, and deadly efficiency in the pursuit of wildlife," extinction rates averaged one species per million each year. Today, however, Wilson warns that extinction rates are "catastrophically high, somewhere between one thousand and ten thousand times the rate before human beings began to exert a significant pressure on the environment." The IUCN concurs with Wilson's assessment, stating in the introduction to the 2004 *Red List* that "people, either directly or indirectly, are the main reason for most species' declines. Habitat destruction and degradation are the leading threats but other significant pressures include over-exploitation for food, pets, and medicine, introduced species, pollution and disease."

Paleontologist Niles Eldredge, who is the curator in chief of the permanent exhibition "Hall of Biodiversity" at the American Museum of Natural History and adjunct professor at the City University of New York, refers to the current loss of species as the "Sixth Extinction," in an article of that title published in June 2001. Eldredge maintains that "there is little doubt left in the minds of professional biologists that Earth is currently faced with a mounting loss of species that threatens to rival the five great mass extinctions of the geological past." Like Edward O. Wilson and the IUCN, Eldredge blames human activity for species endangerment and extinction. He explains that the Sixth Extinction began one hundred thousand years ago when humans began to disperse and settle around the world. Research shows that overhunting by early humans may have been a direct cause of the extinction of several large species of game animals. Moreover, Eldredge points out that humans changed the ecosystem in more subtle ways, through habitat alteration and the introduction of disease.

With the beginnings of agriculture ten thousand years ago, Eldredge maintains that humans began to change the ecosystem even more. As he puts it,

> Agriculture represents the single most profound ecological change in the entire 3.5 billion-year history of life. With its invention:
>
> • humans did not have to interact with other species for survival, and so could manipulate other species for their own use;

- humans did not have to adhere to the ecosystem's carrying capacity, and so could overpopulate.

Eldredge points particularly to the explosion in the human population since the introduction of agriculture as a major factor in the current extinction crisis. Ten thousand years ago between 1 and 10 million people inhabited the planet; today Earth's population has increased to more than 6 billion people. According to Eldredge, overpopulation has resulted in "a vicious cycle":

- More lands are cleared and more efficient production techniques (most recently engendered largely through genetic engineering) to feed the growing number of humans—and in response, the human population continues to expand.

- Higher fossil energy use is helping agriculture spread, further modifying the environment.

- Humans continue to fish (12 of the 13 major fisheries on the planet are now considered severely depleted) and harvest timber for building materials and just plain fuel, pollution, and soil erosion from agriculture creates dead zones in fisheries (as in the Gulf of Mexico).

- The human diaspora has meant the spread, as well, of alien species that more often than not thrive at the detriment of native species. For example, invasive species have contributed to 42% of all threatened and endangered species in the U.S.

Each of these factors, according to Eldredge and other scientists, result from human overpopulation and contribute to ever-growing numbers of animal and plant species becoming threatened, endangered, and eventually extinct.

Not all experts believe that human activity and overpopulation in particular are responsible for the endangered species threat. According to Steven Hayward, Bradley Fellow at the Heritage Foundation, a Washington, D.C.–based think tank, and a senior fellow with the San Francisco–based Pacific Research Institute, a growing population means a growing economy and a healthier environment. Speaking in the 1997 British documentary television program *Against Nature*, Hayward maintains that the advanced technologies afforded by strong economies in highly populated countries such as the United States means "we use less land to produce more food than we used 50 years ago. We're able to use less land precisely because of chemical agriculture and some of the very sophisticated techniques that we have. That allows you to preserve more land for wildlife habitat, for open space, for forests and other purposes."

Jane S. Shaw, a senior associate at the Property and Environment Research Center (PERC) in Bozeman, Montana, points out in her February 2004 article published in the *Backgrounder,* a Heritage Foundation publication, that while human population growth may mean that people will continue to alter the habitats of endangered species, "the new residents will create habitat for wildlife. They will create ponds, establish gardens, plant trees, and set up bird nesting-boxes. Ornamental nurseries and truck farms may replace cropland, and parks may replace hedgerows." Shaw stresses that

> the 21st century is likely to be an environmental century. Affluent people will seek to maintain or, in some cases, restore an environment that is attractive to wildlife, and more parks will likely be nestled within suburban developments, along with gardens, arboreta, and environmentally compatible golf courses. As wildlife proliferates, [people] will learn to live harmoniously with more birds and meso-mammals [mammals of medium size]. New organizations and entrepreneurs will help integrate nature into the human landscape. There is no reason to be pessimistic about the ability of wildlife to survive and thrive.

While there may not be agreement among experts about how and why so many plants and animals are threatened with extinction today, scientists concur that whatever the reason, the list of endangered species is long and growing. A better understanding of the endangered species problem is a vital tool for comprehending the many different aspects of this important issue. *Contemporary Issues Companion: Endangered Species* helps provide that understanding with chapters that explore species extinction, endangered species protection efforts, the debate over the Endangered Species Act, and the challenges faced by wildlife conservation scientists.

CHAPTER 1

# THE PATH TO
# EXTINCTION

Contemporary Issues
Companion

# THE COMING EXTINCTION CRISIS

Janet Larsen

Janet Larsen is a research associate at the Earth Policy Institute in Washington, D.C. In this selection, she relates the consensus among scientists that the earth is experiencing a mass extinction crisis like the one that killed off the dinosaurs 65 million years ago. While previous mass extinctions were caused by geological events, Larsen maintains that the present threat is the result of human activities. An expanding human population has required the clearing of land for agriculture and development. This, coupled with the exploitation of species through hunting and trade, says Larsen, has meant that animal and plant species are currently disappearing faster than at any time in geological history. Larsen stresses that healthy ecosystems are key to the survival of all species, including humans, and that people should act together to halt the progress of this newest mass extinction.

Almost 440,000,000 years ago, some 85% of marine animal species were wiped out in the Earth's first known mass extinction. Roughly 73,000,000 years later, large quantities of fish and 70% of marine invertebrates perished in a second major extinction event. Then, about 245,000,000 years ago, up to 95% of all animals were lost in what is thought to be the worst extinction in history. Approximately 37,000,000 years hence, yet another mass extinction took a toll primarily on sea creatures, but also some land animals. Finally, 65,000,000 years ago, three-quarters of all species—including the dinosaurs—were eliminated.

Among the possible causes of these mass extinctions were volcanic eruptions, falling meteorites, and changing climate. After each extinction, it took upwards of 10,000,000 years for biological richness to recover. Yet, once a species is gone, it is gone for good.

The consensus among biologists is that we now are moving toward another mass extinction that could rival the past big five. This one is unique, however, in that it is largely caused by the activities of a single species. It is the sole mass extinction that humans will witness firsthand—and not just as innocent bystanders.

Janet Larsen, "The Sixth Great Extinction," *USA Today*, vol. 125, November 2004, p. 51. Copyright © 2004 by Society for the Advancement of Education. Reproduced by permission.

# Disappearing Species

While scientists are not sure how many species inhabit the planet today, their estimates top 10,000,000. Each year, though, thousands of species, ranging from the smallest microorganisms to larger mammals, are lost forever. Some disappear even before we know of their existence.

The average extinction rate today is up to 10,000 times faster than the rate that has prevailed over the past 60,000,000 years. Throughout most of geological history, new species evolved faster than existing species disappeared, thus continuously increasing the planet's biological diversity. Now, evolution is falling behind.

Only a small fraction of the world's plant species has been studied in detail, but as many as half are threatened with extinction. South and Central America, Central and West Africa, and Southeast Asia—all home to diverse tropical forests—are losing plants most rapidly. Moreover, nearly 5,500 animal species are known to be threatened with extinction. The International Union for Conservation of Nature and Natural Resources–World Conservation Union's 2003 Red List survey of the world's flora and fauna shows that almost one in every four mammals and one in eight birds are threatened with extinction within the next several decades.

Of 1,130 threatened mammals, 16% are critically endangered—the highest threat level. This means that 184 of their species have suffered extreme and rapid reduction in population or habitat and may not survive the decade. Their remaining numbers range from under a few hundred to, at most, a few thousand. For birds, 182 of the 1,194 threatened species are critically endangered.

Although the status of most of the world's mammals and birds is fairly well-documented, we know relatively little about the rest of the world's fauna. A mere five percent of fish, six percent of reptiles, and seven percent of amphibians have been evaluated. Of those studied, at least 750 fish species, 290 reptiles, and 150 amphibians are at risk. Worrisome signs—like the mysterious disappearance of entire amphibian populations and fishermen's nets that come up empty more frequently—reveal that there may be more species in trouble. Of invertebrates, including insects, mollusks, and crustaceans, we know the least—but what is known is far from reassuring.

# The Human Impact

At the advent of agriculture some 11,000 years ago, the world was home to 6,000,000 people. Since then, our ranks have grown a thousandfold. Yet, the increase in our numbers has come at the expense of many other species.

The greatest threat to the world's living creatures is the degradation and destruction of habitat, affecting nine out of 10 threatened species. Humans have transformed nearly half of the planet's ice-free land areas, with serious effects on the rest of nature. We have made agricultural fields out of prairies and forests. We have dammed rivers and drained wetlands. We have paved over soil to build cities and roads.

Each year, the Earth's forest cover shrinks by 40,000,000 acres, with most of the loss occurring in tropical forests. Ecologically rich wetlands have been cut in half over the past century. Other freshwater and terrestrial ecosystems have been degraded by pollution. Deserts have expanded to overtake previously vegetated areas, accelerated in some cases by overgrazing of domesticated animals.

A study of 173 species of mammals from around the world showed that their collective geographical ranges have been halved over the past several decades, signifying a loss of breeding and foraging area. Overall, between two and 10% of mammal populations (groups of a single species in a specific geographical location) are thought to have disappeared along with their habitat.

Direct human exploitation of organisms, such as through hunting and harvesting, threatens more than one-third of the listed birds and mammals. Other threats to biodiversity include exotic species, often transported by humans, which can outcompete and displace native ones.

A survey of some 1,100 animal and plant species found that climate change could wipe out between 15–37% of them by 2050. Yet, the actual losses may be greater because of the complexity of natural systems. The extinction of key species could have cascading effects throughout the food chain.

## Preventing Extinctions

Healthy ecosystems support us with many services—most fundamentally by supplying the air we breathe and filtering the water we drink. They provide us with food, medicine, and shelter. When ecosystems lose biological richness, they also lose resilience, becoming more susceptible to the effects of climate change, invasions of alien species, and other disturbances.

Consciously avoiding habitat destruction and mitigating the effects of land use alteration, reducing the direct exploitation of plants and wildlife, and slowing climate change can help us stop weakening the very life-support systems we depend on. While this may be the first time in history that a single species can precipitate a mass extinction event, it also is the only time that a single species can act to prevent it.

# HUMANS ARE PRIMARILY RESPONSIBLE FOR SPECIES EXTINCTION

David Watson

David Watson is the author of *Beyond Bookchin: Preface for a Future Social Ecology*. In this selection, Watson argues that the prevailing human attitude that people are the "lords of nature" is the cause of species endangerment and extinction. Watson disagrees with the idea that extinctions are a natural and unavoidable result of human expansion. He states that in many instances humans have ignorantly slaughtered species when such extinction was preventable. Watson insists that human beings should learn to live in a way that leaves the planet in a state of ecological harmony for all species. Making this decision, however, will require humans to limit their own numbers, alter their consumption patterns, and agree to live a more simplified existence.

An optimistic, problem-solving attitude can sometimes conceal a deeper despair. In 1995 India's Environment Ministry moved to protect Indian butterfly and moth species under the Government's Wildlife Act. Sensible enough! The measure came after two German tourists were caught trying to leave the country with 15,000 preserved butterflies and moths in their luggage. Should we feel relief at attempts to plug one of the myriad leaks in nature's troubled reservoir, hope that some at least are grappling with a grave issue most of us did not even suspect existed? Or numb our grief; knowing that the guardians cannot block every gate nor staunch every hemorrhaging wound? "Man the exterminator has designs on everything that lives," the misanthropic philosopher E.M. Cioran once quipped. "Soon we will be hearing about the last louse."

For me these two smugglers exemplify a narrow self-interest driving both individuals and international institutions toward the abyss. But they were the only ones intercepted, not the 50, perhaps even 100 who got away. In a world where humans are the measure of all things and the sole repository of value, every unique manifestation of life be-

David Watson, "Empire of Extinction," *Earth Island Journal*, vol. 19, Autumn 2004.

comes merchandise and rare butterflies have little chance of living out their own evolutionary destiny. Sadly, such macrocosmic insults as dam construction, logging, the use of biocides, and urban sprawl dwarf the collector as a threat to butterflies and their habitat. And as a single moth goes, so may a flower, and other members of a small and complex community of life utterly indivisible, and invisible to us.

## Accelerating Extinctions

Those moths and butterflies that do eventually succumb will join an accelerating *danse macabre* [death dance] of extinction brought about by our clever species during the last few centuries, especially the last few decades. Some victims are already gone: the great auk, passenger pigeon, woodland bison, dodo (and with it the tambalocoque tree, dependent for its germination on the passage of its seed through the dodo's digestive tract). Others are sliding irrevocably toward the chute: rhinoceros, elephant, tiger, piping plover, and countless other creatures vanishing before we even know of them. Like the auk, so utterly extinguished by the mid-1800s that some thought it apocryphal, these creatures will one day be considered as fabulous as we today consider the unicorn. It will matter little to our grandchildren whether they once lived or were mere inventions.

It's easy to find scientists and laypeople who consider this sense of loss mere sentimentality unworthy of our status as "the lords and possessors of nature," to repeat [French philosopher René] Descartes' unhappy phrase. After all, extinction is natural and inevitable, they are quick to remind us. Trying to save species that have lost in the competition between the "fit" and "unfit" is to turn back an inexorable clock. There is little room for such beautiful losers in the ongoing march of progress.

Extinction may be natural. But today countless species are more like the victims of Latin American death-squad regimes, being made actively to "disappear." Rising human population is widely considered an underlying cause of the contemporary die-off along with the bull-dozer's blade and chainsaw's teeth. Ecological collapse is typically represented by a landless peasant slashing the forest with his machete, or a tribal woman carrying a bundle of sticks on her head and a hungry child on her back.

## Too Many People

To be sure, the ascending J-curve of rising human numbers, accompanying the vertiginous obliteration of countless other species, leaves a stunning impression. Yet sheer numbers do not totally explain the current mass-extinction spasm. We need to look beyond the numbers, at social structures, at an energy- and commodity-intensive development model and the social and historical causes of extreme poverty. While they comprise only 25 percent of the world's population, industrial nations account for 75 percent of energy use and consume 85 percent of forest products. US per-capita energy consumption is 250 times greater than in many poor countries. Obviously daily life in the North contributes far more to ecological destruction than population growth in the South. On a global scale, according to one US official, the impact of the world's poorest people is "probably more akin to picking up branches and twigs after commercial chainsaws have done their work."

There is a wide divergence of opinion about planetary carrying capacity and the human numbers that can adequately be supported (though there are copious signs that our ability to feed ourselves is declining due to abuse and over-exploitation of our food sources). But even if some believe we can provide a decent life for twice the number of people now living, no thoughtful person could possibly doubt the disastrous effect such numbers will inevitably have on other species. How many people the earth can support is the wrong question. We also need to think about what kind of life we want: crowded into a megalopolis with a landscape entirely marshalled to meet our ever-expanding needs; or in community with other species in a green world at least something like the one in which we evolved. The latter is the kind of planet that will make it possible for all species to flourish, along with essential wilderness and diverse land and ocean habitats. That will be the best world for us too, but it will necessitate fewer of us.

There is a "nature-red-in-tooth-and-claw" idea that human depredation and consequent mass extinction are entirely natural. According to this view even Palaeolithic humans, being an intrinsically murderous lot, carried out their share of mass extinctions: for example, supposedly wiping out many large mammals in North America. Yet there is little hard evidence, and much reason to doubt—except in obvious cases of extinction on islands, like that of the flightless moa of Aotearoa/New Zealand—that mass extinctions were caused by prehistoric foragers and hunters.

## Human Arrogance

Farley Mowat, in his book *Sea of Slaughter*, gives us a dizzying description of the carnage perpetrated on the animals of the North American eastern seaboard by explorers and entrepreneurs. He points out that the great auk co-existed with human hunters for millennia. But it succumbed in a couple of hundred years to the mechanized, market-driven empire that was only a quaint precursor to our own. We can remain agnostic about whether or not our distant ancestors foolishly fouled their nest. It is pretty much irrelevant to the reality we face now: an immensely brutal and thoroughly anthropocentric civilization ravaging the earth, ostensibly in our interest. The scale and scope of such devastation is unprecedented in the history of our species.

This civilization's arrogance is evident in our scientific tradition's urge to expand what [philosopher] Francis Bacon called "the empire of man." But it goes back even further. The Judaeo-Christian biblical edict granted us "dominion over the fish of the sea, and over the fowl of the air, and over the cattle, and over all the earth, and over every creeping thing that creepeth upon the earth." Now many animals mentioned in the Bible are going the way of the Dodo—Jonah's whale, the Persian wild ass on which Jesus rode into Jerusalem, the Nubian ibex, the Arabian oryx that Isaiah tells us was trapped in nets.

Human dominion has done these creatures little good; most have fallen forever into our nets. The image of a human imperium oppressing the rest of nature is no mere metaphor. It conforms to an actual pattern of imperial conquest, plunder, eventual exhaustion, and collapse. Our century has given a privileged layer of humanity an industrially organized life more opulent, more wasteful yet also more frenetic, alienated, and depressed than that of any ancient hierarch. We've transformed the earth into a giant mine and waste pit, its forests and meadowlands into enormous feedlots for billions of stock animals, its waters into cesspools devoid of life, its skies into orbiting junkyards of contaminated rocket debris. The world's tallest mountains are littered with expedition trash. Ships at sea do not go a single day without seeing plastic garbage. Giant nets 30 miles long drag the oceans killing millions of sea creatures, including birds and mammals. These are simply "by-catch" to be tossed overboard. The whole planet has become a war zone generating a bio-crisis not just for individual species, but for entire webs of life.

## Transforming the Planet

Human beings are now altering the basic physiology of the planet. Industrial smog can be found everywhere over the oceans, and weather patterns are so distorted that climatologists now discuss "climate death." Industrial contamination is pervasive, even in the fat cells of Antarctic penguins. The rain is not only acid but toxic. Whether industrialism warms or cools the atmosphere, its unprecedented chemical experiment threatens to reconfigure life in ways barely imaginable, but undoubtedly for the worse.

All empires turn out to be relatively short-lived enterprises that finally betray their own subjects. Despite its enormous cost to the rest of life, modern civilization has engendered a mode of existence that fails to provide even the barest essentials for a fifth of humanity or to satisfy the fundamental psychic needs of the rest. Strangely, our very anthropocentrism may be our own undoing. Pragmatic self-interest alone should teach us that we must change before nature exacts inevitable revenge. And nothing can be done, North or South, without social strategies that create institutions to provide practical alternatives and thus opportunities for people to change.

Yet meaningful subversion of the "empire of man" requires more than enlightened self-interest or even social justice. It means real transformation, a cultural practice that considers all life a larger community deserving of our solidarity. In the process, people may discover that limiting our numbers and consumption, living more simply so that others (human and non-human) may simply live, brings ineluctable rewards of its own.

Such recognition suggests precisely that spiritual dimension which is missing from modern life and its frenzy of accumulation. For the last few years I have practiced T'ai Chi, an ancient, meditative martial art that names many of its postures for animals such as monkeys, cranes, and tigers. I have often wondered what would become of a practice inextricably woven to such creatures when human hubris finally extinguishes them. What will become of our own spirit when inspirited creatures we invoke are gone from our midst? Who—and what—will we be? When will we realize the life-forms and life-webs we've slaughtered and abused are our own larger self, as many native peoples, radical ecologists, and other "counter-traditions" remind us? Only with this awareness will we begin the necessary process of renewal that could make life worth living in the coming centuries.

# SPECIES CAN RECOVER FROM HUMAN ENCROACHMENT

John Pike

In the following selection, John Pike reveals that, despite warnings of ecological doom, plant and animal species are returning in abundance to the forests of the eastern United States. When settlers first arrived in North America, Pike notes, it took only a short time for forests to be decimated due to timber harvesting and clearing for agriculture. As a result, many animal species were driven away or eliminated entirely. Today, however, forests in the eastern United States are thriving, Pike reports. In addition, animals such as moose, beaver, and bear are returning in increasing numbers. Pike suggests that this environmental resilience means that pessimism about the environment is unfounded. He suggests that people accept the good news that habitats and species can, and do, recover from human activities. Pike is a contributing writer for *Insight on the News* magazine.

By October of 1630 the tadpole-shaped peninsula called Boston had 150 English-speaking residents. Led by John Winthrop, the colony's first governor, these Puritan emigrants virtually began the historical process in which large numbers of recent European arrivals settled and subdued Massachusetts Bay and the North American environment during the next three-and-one-half centuries.

With each austere-living family constructing a wooden home and fencing an adjacent garden, Bostonians by the 1640s already were traversing the Charles River to gather firewood and building materials as precious timber close at hand virtually had been erased. As early as the winter of 1637–38, Winthrop noted, Boston was "almost ready to break up for want of wood."

Peter Dunwiddie, a plant ecologist with the Nature Conservancy in Washington state, has studied core samples of bogs and swamps on Cape Cod, looking at microscopic pollen to determine what was growing there and on the proximate islands about the time the Pilgrims landed in nearby Plymouth, Mass. His research shows the development of English settlements.

"Literally in a matter of decades the forest was cleared," Dunwiddie says. "There is no more oak pollen, and all of a sudden lots of grass pollen. That persisted throughout much of the following couple of hundred years" as Europeans transformed most of the area into a giant sheep pasture. The cleric Timothy Dwight wrote in 1821 that "almost all the original forests of [southern New England] had long since been cut down."

Dwight also reported that the 240-mile journey from Boston to New York City passed through no more than 20 miles of forest. Surveying the changes wrought by farmers and loggers miles upstream from the coast near Dover, N.H., Dwight wrote, "The forests are not only cut down, but there appears little reason to hope that they will ever grow again."

One easily can see evidence today of that deforestation throughout most areas of New England with a short walk in what once more are woods. The ubiquitous rock walls of New England's currently wooded areas mark the edges of erstwhile farms abandoned years ago.

## Altering the Landscape

The widespread deforestation centuries ago was due to farming and wood being used for virtually everything—home construction, of course, but mostly for heating and cooking. According to the U.S. Forest Service (USFS), the amount of forested land in Massachusetts drastically decreased from 4.63 million acres in 1630 to 2 million acres in 1907. Maryland went from 5.73 million acres to 2.2 million acres, Rhode Island from 650,000 acres to 250,000 acres and Delaware from 1.13 million acres to 350,000 acres.

And with the stripping of the forests and increased hunting came a depopulation of the animals that lived among the trees. The environment as a whole was changing radically.

But it was not only the new arrivals from European shores that altered the landscape. American Indians prior to the arrival of the Pilgrims also had a great effect on the land, though not as much on a per capita basis as the new Europeans. Human destruction of the forests did not start with the English, Spanish or French, as the Indian natives affected tens-of-millions of acres. The American forests first seen by the new English colonists in the 17th century were far from primordial.

Doug MacCleery of the USFS in Washington says the American Indians "burned forests to grow crops and create grasslands and prairies to increase the numbers of the game they hunted." Indians also burned down trees to make it easier to travel, create open space around their villages to hinder sneak attacks from their enemies and as a hunting method to drive animals into enclosures, MacCleery says. "There was lots of grassland in Ohio and along the eastern coast as a result of Indian burning."

Indeed, the names given to venues by Indians often had to do with the area's agricultural purposes, which meant clearing trees. According to William Cronon, author of *Changes in the Land*, "Mittineag, in Hampden County, Mass., meant 'abandoned fields,' probably a place where the soil had lost its fertility and a village had moved to its summer encampment elsewhere."

But there was fluctuation. MacCleery adds that because large numbers of Indians tragically died from foreign diseases after the new Europeans first came, many areas of the American environment then were returned to more of a "wilderness" state after most of them perished.

## The Resilience of Nature

As the European population of the newly formed United States increased from the founding of the colonies, the deforestation of the eastern United States reached a peak in the mid-19th century. But it was then that nature demonstrated, once again, just how truly resilient she is. Consider just one small but highly indicative example of it in 1996:

On June 14 of that year a 7-foot, 1,000-pound, young female moose paraded along the major thoroughfare of Commonwealth Avenue in Boston, in proximity to Boston University and Boston College, and just a short subway ride to the spot where the Puritans first landed. Once abundant, the forces set in motion by European colonization erased moose from Massachusetts by the turn of the century. But now the commonwealth has between 50 and 100 moose, with a population breeding in the Boston suburb of Acton. For her sexy, attention-gathering catwalk, Miss Moose was, as surely as John Winthrop, a pioneer.

But what Miss Moose represents is much more than just a large personable ruminant reclaiming her native territory among the cars, factories and apartment buildings of Boston—it demonstrates the most important environmental story of the 20th century. The key event in recent American environmental history is not the Exxon Valdez or the spotted owl, but the vast reforestation of the eastern side of the North American continent. The American East Coast has exploded in green.

In the last few decades, as 19th century farms have been abandoned, the forest cover in the eastern United States has returned abundantly despite its much larger population and increased development of suburban and rural areas. Bill McKibben, author of several environmental books, writes that the forest cover of the eastern United States today is as extensive as it was before the American Revolution. This renewal of the eastern forest largely is the result of economic accident and generally unremarked.

Tom French, of the Massachusetts Division of Fisheries and Wildlife, says the state reached its peak of deforestation about the time of the Civil War, when approximately 70 percent of the forest had been cleared. Virtually the only trees left standing were on precipitous slopes, venues difficult for farming.

## Expanding Forests

Since agriculture no longer dominates either the Massachusetts economy or that of the eastern United States, abandoned farms once again have become forested. French says 62 percent of Massachusetts land now is wooded, a precipitous increase that occurred despite a sixfold growth in the human population. And, according to Dunwiddie's bog cores, "the pollen is now beginning to resemble the pre-European." MacCleery says that the land in Vermont in 1850 was 35 percent forested, whereas today it is 80 percent forested.

A USFS website states that the amount of forest in Pennsylvania grew from 9.2 million acres in 1907 to 16.9 million acres in 1997. New York state jumped from 12 million acres to 18.58 million acres, Rhode Island from 250,000 acres to 409,000 acres and Illinois from 2.5 million acres to 4.29 million acres, all within what could be someone's lifetime.

"Nationally, forest growth rates have exceeded harvest rates since the 1940s," MacCleery states. "The United States in total has about the same area of forests as it did in 1920. The [predicted] timber famine never came." In the Northeast United States, the country's most populous region, MacCleery says the land was less than 50 percent forested in 1900. Today, he says, the region is more than two-thirds forested, an increase of 26 million acres.

## Returning Animals

But the nation's 20th-century environmental progress goes way beyond numbers of trees, for the animals that live in these woods are pouncing forward after taking a severe beating. The almost complete elimination of the East Coast forests in past centuries resulted, among other environmental difficulties, in severely depleting or eliminating many species of animals indigenous to the wooded lands, including white-tailed deer, wolves, fishers, bears, bobcats, beavers and mountain lions. In 1694, Massachusetts established its first closed season on deer hunting, a mere 64 years after Winthrop first landed. And the bears eventually moved out of state. But after all the Massachusetts bear population had vanished, since 1991 state wildlife officials say their numbers have increased from 725 to almost 2,000, with occasional backyard sightings that greatly excite (or scare) homeowners, sometimes within 45 minutes of the Boston Stone at the heart of the old city. Bear numbers in Massachusetts now are equal to those in the 1700s.

Beavers were hunted in colonial Massachusetts for their fur and were disappearing from its coast as early as 1640. They were erased utterly from the commonwealth by 1764 until the early 1900s. But now there are 70,000 of the workaholic rodents laboriously constructing menacing dams throughout the state.

One beaver enjoyed a sunny spring day floating along the Merrimack River in downtown Lowell, adjacent to the Boott Cotton Mills where the American industrial revolution began in the early 1800s. The beaver's neighbors now include Atlantic salmon, which had stopped swimming in the Merrimack years ago when the river became one of the most soiled in the nation. Salmon also now live in the Connecticut River, where just 152 once were estimated.

Although a few animals have not returned from the days of deforestation, many indigenous Massachusetts species are undergoing a startling renaissance. Coyotes now live in virtually every town. They crossed the Cape Cod Canal in the 1970s and started breeding on the Cape. Being good swimmers they recently have made the short ocean crossing to the Elizabeth Islands.

"Today we kill twice as many deer on the highways of America than existed in the entire eastern United States in 1890," MacCleery says. "In 1890, Pennsylvania, Ohio and the lower part of Michigan did not have any deer." Officials estimate Pennsylvania's deer population today is 1.5 million.

"Many species which would likely have been on the endangered species list—had one existed in 1900—are today abundant," MacCleery says, "including wild turkey, beaver, egrets, herons and many other wading birds, wood ducks, whistling swans, Rocky Mountain elk, pronghorn antelope, bighorn sheep, black bear and white-tailed deer." He says, "Many other species, although not on the brink of extinction in 1900, are today both more abundant and more widespread than they were back then."

## Environmental Pessimism

In addition to the added forest area of the eastern United States, the resurgence of many species of animals throughout the last few decades also can directly be attributed to changes in levels of pollution that affect, among other aspects, the manifold varieties of foods animals consume. Here again the news is almost all positive.

Unfortunately, few ideas are more deeply entrenched in our political culture than that of impending ecological doom. Mostly beginning in the early 1960s when warnings from Rachel Carson and others began to emerge that pollution was a threat to all forms of life, pessimistic appraisals of the health of the environment have been issued with increasing urgency. Doomsday warnings led to the first Earth Day demonstrations in 1970, and three significant environmental laws were passed during the Republican administration of Richard Nixon: the Clean Air Act (1970), the Clean Water Act (1972) and the Endangered Species Act (1973).

And what a success the environmental cleanup has been. "The

Clean Air and Clean Water acts led to actions that resulted in substantial environmental gains," MacCleery states in a USFS publication. "Air quality has been steadily improving in U.S. cities. Sulfur-dioxide emissions are down over 30 percent and lead emissions are down over 95 percent since 1970." The Environmental Protection Agency (EPA) website states that "since 1970 aggregate emissions of the six principal pollutants have been reduced by 29 percent. During this same period the U.S. gross domestic product increased 158 percent, energy consumption increased by 45 percent and vehicle miles traveled have increased by 143 percent."

Smog nationally has declined by about one-third, say environmental officials, despite an increase in the number of cars. The number of days in which the health standard for smog is violated has decreased significantly during the last 15 years. The use of unleaded gas has contributed to our cleaner air. Smokestacks belching black smoke in the United States have been eliminated save for when a burner malfunctions.

During the 19th century, respiratory problems were common with the burning of coal and coke and the emission of ammonia. Robert Boisselle, of the Massachusetts Department of Environmental Protection, says, "Massachusetts no longer experiences an occasional dark brown haze due to smog as it did years ago. . . . We can still see some haze occasionally, but nothing like it used to be."

## Cleaner Rivers

So much for doomsday statements by radical environmentalists who continually bark out predictions of increasingly darkened and smelly American skies. What about the rivers?

"Most U.S. rivers and lakes are measurably cleaner than they were two decades ago," MacCleery observes. "Improved air and water quality have benefited both the human and nonhuman inhabitants of the planet, as evidenced by the improving populations of fish and aquatic wildlife in U.S. rivers and lakes. Fish and wildlife have staged significant comebacks in many rivers and lakes that were severely degraded or even biologically dead two decades ago. There have been increases in the populations of egrets, herons, ospreys, geese, large-mouth bass and other fish and wildlife associated with the improved water quality of countless rivers and lakes across the country."

American rivers once were used as sewers. Downstream from 19th century New England textile mills, rivers would change color according to the particular dye being used that day. Poisons and raw sewage commonly were dumped into the rivers. No more. According to the EPA, there now are more than 11,000 miles of streams and rivers in which it again is safe to swim. There are almost 13,000 additional fishable bodies of water and 5,400 added places suitable for boating.

Massachusetts is indicative of the rest of the East Coast, and French says that overall, in terms of what most people believe pollution is, the commonwealth hit a peak of pollution sometime in the first half of the 20th century. Boston Harbor, among the first heavily used harbors in the United States—and attacked by Republicans (unfairly) during the presidential campaign of then-governor Michael Dukakis as being very dirty—has undergone a startling renaissance. "Overall, the water quality of Boston Harbor has greatly improved since the year 1900" says Russell Isaac of the Massachusetts Department of Environmental Protection. "The ability to swim in the harbor has significantly improved" and there is less disease-causing wastewater. "We have made a lot of progress in the overall environment, but more needs to be done" Isaac says.

## Good Environmental News
Nor will the animals we care about need to hightail it to the Canadian border to escape a perceived onslaught of relaxed environmental laws. Newt Gingrich, the former speaker of the House whom many on the left consider to be the reptilian soul of the Republican Party, is an outspoken environmentalist and says of preserving U.S. wildlife, "This is not just about large vertebrates. . . . This is also about the fungi and the various things that produce the medicine of the future." Environmentalism has become a core American political value, close to unassailable even among the most febrile conservatives.

So if the overall environment greatly has improved in the 20th century, and continually gets better, why all the pessimistic assessments of the environment blaring from the media? According to one U.S. environmental official who requested anonymity, "In many cases you have advocacy groups that make money creating the perception of a crisis. It is a conflict industry."

Hmmmmm.

While researching this article, your reporter regularly telephoned the EPA for weeks requesting to speak with someone, anyone, who could highlight the achievements of the agency during the last few decades, all to no avail. And MacCleery has a thought about that too: "Some people" at the EPA, he says, "do not view good news as a positive because it jeopardizes future funding." And with that I will leave you to ponder your clean environment, among the happy deer and bears that have joined you in the back yard of your city apartment.

We must not resist the good news.

# EXOTIC ANIMALS CONTRIBUTE TO THE ENDANGERMENT OF NATIVE SPECIES

Sally Deneen

In the following selection, author Sally Deneen reviews the negative consequences that foreign—or exotic—animal species have had on domestic species in various parts of the United States. As Deneen relates, exotic species have, in some cases, rapidly overtaken habitats and food sources of native species or preyed on native animals for food. Deneen maintains that it would be impossible to eliminate all the exotic species now in America, especially since some, like cats and dogs, are favored pets. But allowing exotic species to go unchecked will surely doom some native species, Deneen emphasizes. Thus, Americans will face difficult decisions in trying to strike a balance to avoid any mass extinctions. Sally Deneen is a freelance writer based in Seattle.

In one corner of the United States, mountain goats traipse across the fragile alpine flowers that speckle the snowline of Washington's craggy Olympic Mountains. They look beautiful, but the goats don't belong there. Seattle newspaperman E.B. Webster and his mountaineer club 80 years ago pushed to introduce the shaggy-bearded animals to the majestic mountains to boost tourism. So a dozen goats arrived, and the numbers quickly grew to a high of 1,200.

Meanwhile, wolves are native to the same mountains of Olympic National Park, but don't expect to hear their nocturnal howls anytime soon. Neighbors objected when rangers proposed reintroducing the park's missing predator a few years ago. To some, it's simple: alien goats, OK; native wolves, not OK.

In the opposite corner of the country, native animals of the Florida Keys face a public relations problem of their own. At the tony Ocean Reef Resort in Key Largo, hundreds of feral cats are fed by residents at two dozen designated feeding stations—yet the cats are helping kill off the endangered Key Largo cotton mouse. Farther down the island chain, the federal government has forced builders to stop projects in

Sally Deneen, "Going, Going . . . Exotic Species Are Decimating America's Native Wildlife," E, The Environmental Magazine, vol. 13, May/June 2002, p. 34. Copyright © 2002 by Earth Action Network, Inc. Reproduced by permission.

the path of the endangered Lower Keys marsh rabbit. But the feds are virtually powerless when it comes to protecting the rabbits from residents' free-ranging house cats, dogs and those ubiquitous suburban freeloaders, raccoons, which are among the rabbits' other threats, according to the U.S. Army Corps of Engineers.

And while the world's 800 remaining tiny endangered Key deer certainly score as high as Bambi in public appeal, people may love them too much. Illegal feedings cause deer to lose their fear of people and look for food in neighborhoods, where some deer are attacked and killed by dogs. What is wrong with this picture?

## Species Havoc

Throughout the country, it's a similar story: Whether we're aware of it or not, we subtly—and sometimes not so subtly—change the natural world by our choices of which animals we like and don't like. Explorer Hernando de Soto liked hogs and brought 13 with him to Florida in 1539; by 1993 more than two million feral hogs were uprooting untold acres of plants in 23 states and preying on forest birds, yet delighting game hunters, according to federal reports. Fans of the hog in Louisiana have gone so far as to establish the Wild Boar Conservation Association, which encourages the establishment of boar breeding programs.

Collector Eugene Schieffelin is believed to have set free a few dozen starlings in New York's Central Park in March 1890 to introduce the nation to the birds he read about in Shakespeare. Now, their descendents snack at backyard bird feeders and aggressively evict flickers, bluebirds and other natives from their nests across the nation—just as house sparrows, introduced in 1853, harass native robins and displace bluebirds, purple martins and cliff swallows from their nesting sites, according to a 1999 Cornell University report.

Indeed, as the human population grows and people move into new areas, they help transform the landscape by bringing along backyard bird feeders and favorite companions: cats, dogs, reptiles and exotic fish (some of which end up in canals and lakes when aquarium enthusiasts tire of them). Meanwhile, creatures that benefit from living around people follow them into disturbed areas, including opossums, raccoons, pigeons and dumpster-diving rats.

White-tailed deer and coyotes spread into new areas as they take advantage of the disappearance of animals people don't like, such as wolves and grizzly bears. Coyotes now live in every state except Hawaii, and they even snack at outdoor pet-food bowls in cities such as Denver, Los Angeles, Phoenix and New York. Coyotes can eat "doughnuts and sandwiches, pet cats and cat food, pet dogs and dog food, carrion and just plain garbage," according to a 2001 U.S. Department of Agriculture (USDA) report. More coyotes now exist than before the U.S. Constitution was signed, due to an amazingly adaptable scavenger diet and the disappearance of competing wolves.

The nation's big predators are largely gone, notes John Morrison, acting director of the World Wildlife Fund's (WWF) conservation science program. "We, *Homo sapiens*, have arrived and marked our territory well," says Harvard biologist E.O. Wilson in his [2002] book, *The Future of Life*. People have "reshaped the U.S. because somehow we as a species wanted it that way. We chose starlings and gypsy moths and honeybees just as clearly as we chose the Grand Coulee Dam and the Sears Tower," Kim Todd argues in *Tinkering with Eden: A Natural History of Exotics in America*.

Upset upon learning in 1995 that the ivorybill woodpecker had gone extinct after being reduced to the few remaining primeval swamps of Louisiana, Florida and South Carolina, Wilson laments what we are doing to the landscape. "Winners of the Darwinian lottery . . . we are chipping away the ivory-bills and other miracles around us. As habitats shrink, species decline wholesale in range and abundance," Wilson notes. "Being distracted and self-absorbed, as is our nature, we have not yet fully understood what we are doing."

## Mass Extinctions

Biologists are noticing, however, and seven out of 10 say we are in the midst of a "mass extinction" of living things, according to a 1998 survey of 400 biologists commissioned by New York's American Museum of Natural History. One in eight known bird species around the world face a high risk of extinction in the near future, according to the authoritative 2000 International Union for Conservation of Nature and Natural Resources (IUCN) Red List of Threatened Species. That means entire species of birds face the same odds of disappearing from the planet for good as a woman in the U.S. does of developing breast cancer sometime in her lifetime. Mammals have it worse: One in four known mammals worldwide face a high risk of extinction in the near future.

Not since dinosaurs vanished 65 million years ago have so many species disappeared so quickly. And this time, it's mainly due to human activity and not natural phenomena like a comet smashing into the planet, say the polled biologists. They consider biodiversity loss a more serious environmental problem than global warming, pollution or depletion of the ozone layer. In the world's 4.5 billion years, there have been five mass extinctions. The sixth—and fastest—is under way, say biologists.

It may seem like no big deal to lose Florida's humble Ponce de Leon beach mouse, which has vanished due to "real estate development, and perhaps predation by domestic cats," as the IUCN Red List put it. But these very factors—habitat loss and introduction of exotic species—are among the main causes of our current global extinction crisis, biologists say.

"Many wonderful creatures will be lost in the first few decades of the 21st century unless we greatly increase levels of support, involvement and commitment to conservation," says Russell A. Mittermeier, president of Conservation International. Though most of those species live in more biologically diverse regions near the equator, the fact remains that about 280 out of 808 known extinctions have occurred in the U.S., WWF's Morrison points out.

And 42 percent of the nation's threatened or endangered species— both animals and plants—face trouble primarily because of competition with and being killed by non-native species, according to a 1999 Cornell University report. The report's lead author, David Pimentel, says he has found no reason for optimism since 1999. "More foreign species arrive each year," says Pimentel, professor of insect ecology and agricultural sciences. "I do not believe that we are winning the war on exotic species because of increased trade, increased number of people traveling, and the growing human population in the U.S. and world."

## What Was Lost

To get a sense of what is being lost, let's look at the continent that explorers Meriwether Lewis and William Clark saw when they took their arduous journey up the Missouri River to the Pacific Ocean, starting in 1804. Fewer people lived in the entire nation in 1804 than currently live in New York City alone. "It's a marvelous example to show how things have changed," says Chris Dionigi, assistant director for Domestic Policy, Science and Cooperation for the National Invasive Species Council. And it's also a dramatic illustration of humankind's ability to remake the landscape, usually to its detriment.

The explorers saw their first American bison, also known as buffalo, in June 1804 at the mouth of the Kansas River, near today's Missouri/Kansas state border. Clark couldn't believe the number of buffalo he saw feeding on the plain near the mouth of the White River in current-day South Dakota.

Bison were so plentiful above the Milk River in current-day Montana that "the men frequently throw sticks and stones at them to drive them out of their way." At the mouth of the Yellowstone River, "The whole country was covered with herds of buffaloe, Elk & Antelopes," the wowed explorers reported, according to *The Way to the Western Sea* by David Lavender. "The bald Eagle are more abundant here than I ever observed them," Lewis wrote in April 1805.

Grizzly bears occasionally scared the wits out of the explorers in current-day Montana and the Dakotas, and Lewis hotfooted for safety as a badly wounded grizzly pursued him for 70 yards near the mouth of the Yellowstone River.

Clark was impressed when a team member later shot what he thought must be "the largest Bird of North America." It proved to be a California condor (today, among the world's rarest birds). Throughout their trek, the men saw lots of otter, raccoon and birds such as trumpeter swans (today, the world's rarest swan). They became the first naturalists to describe several animals, including the coyote, kit fox, Oregon bobcat and the wolf of the plains, according to [Raymond Darwin] Burroughs [editor of *The Natural History of the Lewis and Clark Expedition*].

## The Beginnings of Change

What Lewis and Clark found on their historic trek has filled entire volumes, but at least two things are clear. The West obviously changed since 1804, as cities sprang up, railroads ferried hunters within easy shooting distance of trophy buffalo, and grizzlies and wolves were pushed into smaller and smaller areas. Secondly, and more surprisingly: Even in 1804, the explorers saw signs that man already had tinkered with the natural world.

The horses that galloped past them descended from horses brought over by Spanish conquistadors. North America's native horse went extinct 10,000 years ago. Dogs, meanwhile, weren't just companions for Native Americans, they were food. Hungry and fatigued, the explorers resorted to buying Native American dogs. "Clark, at least, could not overcome a sense of revulsion at being obliged to eat them," Burroughs wrote.

By the 1940s, red and gray wolves—once found throughout most of North America—vanished from most of the lower 48 states. Grizzlies—which once roamed the western half of North America—today number around 1,000 in the contiguous U.S. They're gone from the Bitterroot Mountains, where Lewis and Clark found healthy populations, but they remain in mountains in Wyoming, Washington, Montana and Idaho, according to the National Wildlife Federation. The U.S. Fish and Wildlife Service was poised to return grizzlies to the Selway-Bitterroot region of central Idaho and northwestern Montana, to the delight of conservationists who pushed for the plan. But Interior Secretary Gale Norton overturned that decision [in 2001].

Fast-forward to today, and more than 50,000 species of exotic animals and plants now live in the United States, Pimentel reports, including about 20 introduced mammals such as dogs and cats (population 66 million and 73 million, respectively). Clearly, we can't re-create the North America that Lewis and Clark found. We've not only introduced new animals and plants, but we've also inalterably paved and built on vast expanses of former wilderness. The nation's human population now approaches 280 million—overwhelming numbers when compared to the roughly six million who lived here during Lewis and Clark's trip.

## Behavioral Change

Still, we're going to have to decide together how to manage these changes, and ask ourselves: Are we trying to return the natural order, and especially our wildlife, to as close to pre-Pilgrim days as possible?

Are we trying to bring back the "good species" and repress the "bad species"? Do we have a moral obligation to preserve as many native animals as possible? If so, what changes could that mean to our daily habits, and are we ready to try them?

Flushable cat litter, for instance, may be killing California sea otters, according to a February 2001 report in *The Scientist*. As the waste goes down the toilet and eventually ends up in the ocean, so can go *Toxoplasma gondii*, a parasite whose only known hosts are felines, including housecats, bobcats, cougars and stray cats. Another parasite under suspicion for otter deaths is *Sarcocystis neurona*, whose only definitive host is the opossum. Close to 40 percent of otter deaths are blamed on diseases such as these. Only about 2,000 otters remain. "It's a serious issue," says marine biologist Jim Curland, a marine program associate for Defenders of Wildlife. "It says what we're doing on land can have some serious repercussions for animals in the ocean."

Around the country, there are other skirmishes that pit native creatures against what may be your favorite animals. In Hawaii, cats and dogs as well as the imported mongoose have seriously affected nesting waterbirds and two seabirds—the dark-rumped petrel and Newell's shearwater, according to the National Biological Service. Several new projects aim to curb predators, and more baby petrels have survived since a program began in the nesting areas at Haleakala National Park on Maui.

Elsewhere, dogs accompanied by their owners happily ran leash-free along a vast expanse of beach at San Francisco's Fort Funston park—that is, until officials determined that one of California's two Bank Swallow coastal communities used 10 acres of the beach. The Golden Gate National Recreation Area closed the 10 acres to dogs to protect the swallow. That prompted a lawsuit from a dog-loving group called Fort Funston Dog Walkers.

## The Cat Problem

Free-roaming cats, thought to live in a newly constructed subdivision in California's Marin County, are showing up at Cemetery Marsh, a 50-acre spot used as a nesting area and over-wintering site by belted kingfishers and snowy egrets, according to the Marin Audubon Society, which is encouraging residents to keep cats indoors. Feral cats, meanwhile, are pitted against California Quail at Bidwell Park in Chico, California, and against rare ground-nesting birds such as California black rail and Western snowy plover at California's East Bay Regional Park District. Animal rights activists object to euthanizing stray and feral cats at either place. In what is viewed as a success story, Chico residents started the Chico Cat Coalition, removed at least 440 cats, found homes for most and sent about 50 cats unsuitable for adoption to live out their days in an enclosed barn on private property. California quail are once again seen at the park, and it's unusual to see a stray cat, according to the American Bird Conservancy, which since 1997 has run a national Cats Indoors! campaign.

Exactly how many animals are killed by cats is hotly contested. Based on studies in Wisconsin and Virginia, Pimentel extrapolated that each free-roaming cat nationally kills five birds per year. So, his report estimates that about 465 million birds are killed nationally each year. Nonsense, counters groups such as Alley Cat Allies, a national feral-cat organization that maintains habitat destruction—not cats—is a far bigger problem. More than 60 studies on feral cats from various continents make three points, according to Alley Cat Allies: Cats are opportunistic and eat what is most easily available. Cats can prey on animals without destroying them. And "cats are rodent specialists. Birds make up a small percentage of their diet when they rely solely on hunting for food."

"It gets really sensitive when you start talking about cats and dogs and things like that. But feral cats and dogs can cause quite a problem," says the Invasive Species Council's Dionigi. If Bruce Coblentz had his way, feral cats would be killed, period. "If it didn't have a tag and it didn't have a home, I'd kill it in a heartbeat. It'd be no different than stepping on a cockroach. It's not to say I'm a cat hater," says Coblentz, a cat owner and professor of wildlife ecology at Oregon State University.

Cats are sort of a "third rail" topic among cat lovers, says WWF's Morrison. Some animal rights groups favor feral cat colonies—designated areas where feral cats are returned after neutering, spaying and vaccinations so they can live out their days outside.

But Morrison and Coblentz say it isn't humane for the native animals killed by feral cats. "You would think people would be advocating for the safety and well-being of native species," Morrison says.

In the end, we're left with troubling questions about how to try to reverse the world's fastest extinction rate of animals and plants since dinosaurs roamed the Earth. Is it more humane to kill every last feral hog or round up every feral cat in order to help natives? Or is it more humane to let them live at the expense of natives, such as the Key Largo cotton mouse? The danger is that instead of pondering difficult questions and coming up with our own solutions, we may opt to play a game of cat and mouse with the truth.

# CHAPTER 2

# THE IMPACT OF
# THE ENDANGERED
# SPECIES ACT

Contemporary Issues
Companion

# DELAYS IN IMPLEMENTING AND REAUTHORIZING THE ENDANGERED SPECIES ACT

Brian Lavendel

In the following selection, Brian Lavendel, a freelance author and contributing editor for *Animals*, discusses the history and future of the Endangered Species Act (ESA). When the ESA was passed in 1973, it gave the U.S. government the responsibility to protect threatened or endangered plants and animals. However, Lavendel notes that conflicts between scientists, businesses, and landowners have made it difficult to designate a species as endangered or threatened. Therefore, many disappearing species are not being protected by the ESA. Moreover, Lavendel continues, a critical lack of funding to implement the ESA makes protecting endangered species even more difficult. Despite these drawbacks, Lavendel reports, conservationists believe that if the public is educated about the importance of the ESA, it will ultimately be reauthorized.

The southwestern willow flycatcher is a small, grayish green bird with a whitish throat and a light gray-olive breast. But if you ask Peter Galvin for a description, he'll tell you the bird is invisible. Galvin, a conservation biologist and cofounder of the Center for Biological Diversity, has yet to see a southwestern willow flycatcher in the wild, although he thinks he may have heard the bird call.

Galvin has scoured New Mexico's rough terrain for a sign of the rare bird for the last 10 years. His boots tell the tale of countless treks up and down the sunbaked gravel and silt of the Gila's riverbed. But despite his wide-ranging quest, "I didn't find a one," he concedes. Not a surprising result, perhaps, since only 300 to 500 of the birds are left in the wild.

What he did find may explain the bird's scarcity. "We saw hundreds of miles of streams that were no longer streams," he reports. The small forest groves that grew along those streams—once prime habitat for the willow flycatcher—were disappearing,

In the arid Southwest, streams are "rivers of life." Today, though, much of their flow is diverted to urban centers and agriculture. "They're pumping water for growing iceberg lettuce in the desert," exclaims Galvin. Tapping underground aquifers and streambeds lowers the water table "to the point where trees can no longer reach the water and they die," he says.

But Galvin wasn't about to give up on the southwestern willow flycatcher, and he made it his mission to prod the government into enforcing the Endangered Species Act (ESA).

The ESA, a groundbreaking law signed by President Nixon on December 28, 1973, calls for the U.S. government to bear the responsibility of "safeguarding, for the benefit of all citizens, the Nation's heritage in fish, wildlife, and plants." Under the act, the government or any citizen group has the power to petition that a species be considered as a candidate for listing as "endangered" or "threatened." Once a species is listed, the U.S. Fish and Wildlife Service (USFWS) is required to develop a plan for conservation and recovery of the species and designate habitat critical to its survival. Today the ESA is the major tool in species protection in the United States and a model for wildlife conservation around the globe. "Without the act, hundreds or even thousands of species would be extinct," asserts Galvin. "It's nature's last line of defense."

## Politics and the ESA

But despite the act's broad vision, it hasn't lived up to its potential, argue some wildlife biologists. Science is supposed to be the determining factor in listing and in important decisions, but economic interests, they say, have gradually diminished the political will to implement the visionary law. As Galvin puts it: "The most important wildlife law in the world is being consistently undermined by powerful interests. Every step of the way, you have a politicization of the process."

On the other side are industries such as loggers, land developers, and motorized recreation as well as some private landowners. They complain that the ever-growing list of endangered and threatened species imposes unfair burdens on them and leads to lost jobs.

Attempts to protect the snail darter, the two-inch fish that held up the construction of the Tellico Dam, and the northern spotted owl, which stood between logging companies and old-growth forests in the Northwest, spurred bitter fights. Politicians and bureaucrats responded by backing away from fully enforcing the ESA.

During the Clinton administration, the ecosystem approach was emphasized over single-species conservation, and compromises in how to apply the ESA were introduced. Special local circumstances were allowed to influence how the law is applied. A "no surprises" rule was adopted to reassure landowners that they would not face unforeseen costs and restrictions on their property; the goal was to encourage conservation agreements. "Safe harbor" agreements allowed landowners to take voluntary steps to improve a species while avoiding any future penalties for undoing them. A low priority was placed on critical-habitat designations. Preference was given to assigning threatened designations over endangered ones. Incidental-take permits [permits that authorize activities that may result in inadvertent harm to an endangered species] began to soar, with 492 issued as of August 2001. Such measures satisfied neither ESA critics nor conservationists.

## Fighting for Species Protection

While studying the endangered Mexican spotted owl for the U.S. Forest Service in eastern Arizona, Galvin found that logging and ranching seemed to take precedence over protection of imperiled species. Would such special-interest meddling force the southwestern willow flycatcher into extinction? To prevent this, Galvin's group filed a series of lawsuits. "We had to go to court every step of the way," recalls Galvin. Finally, four years after the initial petition to the government to protect the species, it was officially listed as endangered in 1995.

But it wasn't enough simply to get the bird listed. Conservationists had to make sure that the ESA was actively enforced. Ranchers were grazing cattle along stream banks. The Air Force wanted to conduct low-level flight training over the Gila National Forest. Timber companies had their eyes on logging the streamside forests. And water managements authorities were trying to dam and channel more water to agribusiness and urban centers. Any of these activities had the potential to harm the flycatcher's already decimated habitat, argued Galvin, adding that the Center for Biological Diversity is doing the job the USFWS was charged with.

Bonnie Burgess, who teaches wildlife conservation at Johns Hopkins University, agrees that the USFWS has failed in its enforcement obligations under the ESA. Unfortunately, she says, "it's easy to ignore it—even if it's the law of the land."

## A Critical Lack of Funding

Burgess, author of *Fate of the Wild: The Endangered Species Act and the Future of Biodiversity*, says that even when the USFWS recognizes a species' extinction risk, it often lacks the money and staff to follow up with the necessary research. More than 287 animals and plants are awaiting USFWS decisions on whether they should be listed under the ESA. Meanwhile, of 1,249 species on the endangered and threatened lists, only 78 percent have approved recovery plans, and a mere 12 percent have had critical habitat designated by the agency.

"There is almost unanimous concurrence that the ESA has always been underfunded," points out Mike Senatore, legal director for Defenders of Wildlife. "The statute has never been funded at a level that would allow the USFWS to do what it needs."

The funding issue came to a head in November 2000 when the US-FWS, announcing a moratorium on new listings of endangered species and on the designation of critical habitat, placed a large share of the blame on the many lawsuits the agency has been forced to contend with. "[We do] not have any remaining resources or staff to place new species on the list of threatened and endangered species or to respond to citizen petitions to list new species," asserted Gary Frazer, assistant director for endangered species, in testimony before the U.S. Senate in May 2001.

Conservationists bristled at the accusation that legal actions were behind the USFWS's ESA failures. Lobbyists hostile to the ESA were hampering full implementation, they charged, by convincing legislators to squeeze the USFWS budget. "Opponents of the Endangered Species Act have been waging an underhanded war for years by not allocating money for endangered-species protection," says Brock Evans, executive director of the Endangered Species Coalition, a nonprofit representing more than 430 conservation, scientific, business, religious, and environmental organizations.

Getting full funding, however, is a pipe dream in these days of war and recession. The USFWS estimates that it will require at least $120 million to process the backlog of species and habitats in need of protection, yet its 2002 budget stands at only $8.47 million.

USFWS officials such as Chris Tollefson believe that the money spent fighting lawsuits could be put to better use getting new species listed and working with landowners to recover species that are already on the list. Conservationists counter that the agency shouldn't be able to pick and choose how it enforces the law and that fully funding the ESA would be money well spent.

In August [2002] the USFWS ended its listing moratorium with a historic agreement brokered with three environmental groups—the Center for Biological Diversity, the Southern Appalachian Biodiversity Project, and the California Native Plant Society—to protect 29 imperiled species.

Under the agreement, the USFWS will immediately review three species for emergency listing, issue 14 final listing decisions and eight proposed listing rules, and make decisions on four ESA petitions. The USFWS will also map out critical-habitat areas for the Gila chub, a small-finned, deep-bodied member of the minnow family found in New Mexico and Arizona, and for four freshwater snails in New Mexico.

The species covered by the agreement face significant threats, observers agree. For example, the USFWS will consider emergency listing for the Tumbling Creek cavesnail, which is found in a single cave in Missouri, and the pygmy rabbit in Washington. The agreement also calls for the USFWS to determine whether the Mississippi gopher frog, which occupies one remaining site in Harrison County, Mississippi, should be added to the endangered-species list.

## Battles in Congress

Budget sheets and courtrooms aren't the only battlegrounds for the ESA: there's also Congress. Riders to spending legislation are a favorite weapon for those seeking to circumvent the law's provisions. [In 2002] a proposal conservationists dubbed "the extinction rider" was slipped into President Bush's budget proposal to Congress. This add-on to the Interior Department's appropriations legislation would have eliminated citizen rights to petition that the government protect a threatened or endangered species or bring lawsuits. It also would have removed many of the law's listing deadlines and left listing decisions solely in the hands of the secretary of the Interior. The political end-run was fought off, but many observers fear that other riders will weaken the ESA.

Senator Ted Stevens of Alaska attached a rider to the Interior appropriations bill that would allow cruise ship traffic to rise sharply in Glacier Bay; this could adversely affect humpback whales and other marine mammals. Another rider would allow the Bureau of Land Management to extend lease permits for grazing on public land without the environmental reviews currently mandated by federal law. Two endangered species—the pallid sturgeon and the interior least tern—and the threatened Great Plains piping plover stand to lose out to a rider attached to the House energy and water appropriations bill; this proposal would bar consideration of the USFWS's biological opinion in the management of Missouri River water levels. The list goes on.

On a broader scale, . . . Congress may soon consider whether to reauthorize and amend the entire ESA. Although the law has remained in force and Congress has appropriated money in each fiscal year to implement it—at least partially—authorization for spending under the ESA expired in 1992. Will an updated version minimize regulatory impacts or strengthen the protection it offers to struggling animals and plants? Should the changes in regulations that began in the Clinton administration and are being taken further under Bush be written directly into the law? Will citizen participation be encouraged? The debate is sure to be contentious.

## Educating People About Endangered Species

If conservationists are to win the ESA they want, they will have to build more public support for species protection. That, says Burgess, will take a massive education project—and it won't happen overnight.

She says any successful efforts to protect endangered species will entail changes in our lifestyles, our approach to economics, and even our view of humankind's place in the universe: "It's going to take a deep change in our public attitude to believe that we are not masters of nature—we are just part of it."

The National Wildlife Federation's John Kostyack agrees. Effective species protection will require "a large-scale education process to make people think about the consequences of our behavior and understand why we ought to go to extra trouble to protect plants and animals. . . . This is important not just to wildlife and plants but to our quality of life and our own economic well-being," he says. The good news is that such a change, though gradual, is occurring, according to Kostyack.

[Since 1988], 250 North American animals and plants have gone extinct, some while awaiting ESA protection. Since the act came on the scene, 7 listed species have been lost and 11 recovered enough to be delisted, including the peregrine falcon, American alligator, and brown pelican. If we take the right steps at the right time, species can and do bounce back. Galvin remembers hiking the Gila in 1993, shortly after a massive flood. Streamside vegetation came back stronger than ever, he says. And although Galvin didn't see the southwestern willow flycatcher on that hike either, he takes some solace in knowing the bird is hanging on.

Without the ESA, "the willow flycatcher would almost certainly be extinct," says Galvin. "The Endangered Species Act is a pretty powerful commitment to the planet. It's one of the few laws that says we value nonhuman life." The question is, Do we, as a nation, have the political will to follow through?

# THE ENDANGERED SPECIES ACT RANKS NATURE ABOVE PEOPLE

Michael S. Coffman

Michael S. Coffman is the president of Environmental Perspectives, Inc., a consulting firm that focuses on providing solutions to environmental problems. In the following selection, Coffman argues that the Endangered Species Act (ESA)—the law that protects endangered and threatened species—hurts people by putting the needs of plants and animals before the needs of humans. Individuals have lost land and money because conservation scientists deliberately use bad data to determine which species are endangered, Coffman contends. In addition, the author asserts that conservationists believe that the rights of nature to be undisturbed by "unnatural" human activities are superior to the rights of people to use the land. Furthermore, Coffman points out that the ESA circumvents the U.S. Constitution by allowing the federal government to take private land without compensating the owners in order to protect endangered organisms. He asserts that requiring compensation would force the agencies responsible for implementing the ESA to protect only those species that are truly in need of protection.

Fourteen hundred farmers owning 200,000 acres in the Klamath River Basin of southern Oregon and Northern California were denied their water rights during the summer of 2001 because of the Endangered Species Act of 1973 (ESA). Nearly $200 million of life savings and hard work were wiped out instantly as the farmers were left with essentially worthless land. They are not alone. This has been the legacy of the ESA from its inception. It has confiscated billions of dollars of private property, harmed or destroyed the lives of hundreds of thousands of Americans and has not saved one endangered species! Not one.

The Klamath River incident reveals a glaring problem of the ESA—the lack of or misuse of science. On March 20, 2002, Rob Gordon, Executive Director of the National Wilderness Institute (NWI), testified before the House Resources Committee on H.R. 2829 and H.R. 3705 that would amend the Endangered Species Act of 1973. In addressing the issues of quality of research used, Gordon testified:

> Under the current program the evidentiary standards for listing are, in a word, bad. I use the word bad because it is an apt acronym for "best available data." The problem with best available data, or BAD, is that best is a comparative word. Thus the data need not be verified, reliable, conclusive, adequate, verifiable, accurate or even good.

## Scientific Doubt

The NWI conducted a study in which they found that over 306 of the 976 recovery plans for species listed as endangered had "little to no hard information about the status of listed species." For instance, the plan for the endangered Cave Crayfish cites "Sufficient data to estimate population size or trends is lacking." If there is not even sufficient data to estimate the population size, let alone trends, then how could the USFWS even know it was endangered in the first place? How could it write a recovery plan? The agency could not have. But it did anyway.

With this type of doubt, Secretary of Interior Gale Norton commissioned The National Academy of Sciences (NAS) to investigate the scientific basis for the recovery plans of the suckerfish in the Klamath River Basin. The NAS reported in March of 2002 that there was no scientific justification for keeping Klamath Lake levels high by withholding its water from the farmers. On the contrary, U.S. Fish and Wildlife Service (USFWS) records reveal that the sucker populations increased when the Klamath Lake was low and decreased when it was high. Consequently, the USFWS recovery plan would actually put the suckerfish in greater danger by maintaining high lake levels! And they knew it!

Worse, government scientists are not above actually planting evidence to support their anti-human beliefs. In the fall of 2001, the U.S. Forest Service found that seven federal and state wildlife biologists planted false evidence of a rare and threatened Canadian lynx in the Wenatchee and Gifford Pinchot National Forests in the state of Washington.

Had the fraud gone undetected, it would have closed roads to vehicles. They would have banned off-road vehicles, snowmobiles, skis and snowshoes, livestock grazing and tree thinning. Representatives Richard Pombo (R-California) and John Peterson (R-Pennsylvania) released a joint statement in which they were especially critical of the incident:

> As Americans, we should have been astounded by the recent findings that federal officials intentionally planted hair from the threatened Canadian lynx in our national forests in order to impose sweeping land regulations.

## The Superiority of Nature

None of the seven scientists received any disciplinary action other than a hand slapping and reassignment to another project. Retired Fish and Wildlife Service biologist James M. Beers called the false sampling amazing but not very surprising. "I'm convinced that there is a lot of that going on for so-called higher purposes." This higher purpose is the nature-knows-best theology of conservation biology. Untested, conservation biology is rooted in the religion of pantheism where all human use and activity should follow natural patterns within relatively homogenous soil-vegetation-hydrology landscapes called ecosystems.

Such belief holds that the government should not permit unnatural human development like roads, and activities snowmobiling, livestock grazing and harvesting. Furthermore, ecosystems cross unnatural property, county and state lines. Since conservation biology ostensibly calls for holistic management of entire ecosystems to protect the perceived fragile web of life, the rights of nature must be superior to the rights of people, including their property rights.

The religious zealousness driving the ESA has become so prevalent that David Stirling, Vice-president of the Pacific Legal Foundation wrote in 2002 that:

> For three decades, environmental purists have actively promoted the pantheistic notion that plant and animal life rank higher on the species hierarchy than people. Their "return-to-the-wild" agenda argues that human life activities are the enemy of plant and animal species, and only through their efforts to halt growth and shut down people's normal and necessary life endeavors will Mother Earth smile again.

Federal environmental regulations like the ESA have destroyed the lives of tens of thousands of people, closed entire communities, and confiscated hundreds of millions (if not billions) of dollars of private property—all in the name of protecting the environment. Michael Kelley of the *Washington Post* Writers Group describes the brutality of the ESA in the July 11, 2001, issue of *MSNBC:*

> The Endangered Species Act . . . has been exploited by environmental groups who have forged from it a weapon in their agenda to force humans out of lands they wish to see returned to a pre-human state. Never has this been made more nakedly, brutally clear than in the battle of Klamath Falls.

## Circumventing the Constitution

Congress could not pass the ESA using the Constitutional powers of Article 1, Section 8. Instead, they used five international treaties and Article VI of the U.S. Constitution. The ESA even extols the fact that it cedes sovereignty to the international community by saying its purpose is to "develop and maintain conservation programs which meet national and international standards." In a very real way, U.S. citizens are going to prison, paying thousands of dollars in fines and, in some cases, stripped of their life savings because of international treaties.

Because the legal basis of the ESA rests in international law, it has trumped the Fifth Amendment to the U.S. Constitution. The Fifth Amendment supposedly protects a landowner from a "taking" by the government for public use without just compensation. While the ESA defines "harm" to mean "harass, harm, pursue, hunt, shoot, wound, kill, trap, capture, or collect, or to attempt to engage in any such conduct," for decades, federal agencies arbitrarily extended the definition to take private property to protect the species habitat. The U.S. Supreme Court legitimized this convoluted interpretation on June 29, 1995 in *Babbit v. Sweet Home Chapter of Communities for a Great Oregon.* In doing so, the Court ruled that the word "take" included altering the habitat of an endangered species—thereby allowing the government to take private land for an endangered species without paying for it.

Chief Justice Rehnquist, Justice Scalia and Justice Thomas dissented from the majority ruling; Scalia writing:

> I think it unmistakably clear that the legislation at issue here (1) forbade the hunting and killing of endangered animals, and (2) provided federal lands and federal funds for the acquisition of private lands, to preserve the habitat of endangered animals. The Court's holding that the hunting and killing prohibition incidentally preserves habitat on private lands imposes unfairness to the point of financial ruin—not just upon the rich, but upon the simplest farmer who finds his land conscripted to national zoological use.

Tragically, Scalia was correct. Writing for the Heritage Foundation on November 18, 1998, Alexander Annett notes that: "Because of the Supreme Court ruling, the ESA empowers the federal government to regulate any land that is thought to provide 'suitable habitat' for an endangered species—without proof of death or injury to an identifiable animal that was caused by the landowners." As evidenced in Klamath Falls, zealous bureaucrats can impose arbitrary and capricious habitat recovery plans on private property that instantly strips the value—often their life savings—from a landowner.

## A Recipe for Failure

The purpose of the ESA is to prevent species from becoming extinct and then to help them recover to the point where they no longer need protection. Yet, because landowners face economic ruin if someone finds an endangered species on their land, the landowner is motivated to destroy any habitat or otherwise keep the endangered species off their land before someone finds it. It is a recipe for failure.

Of the sixty species that have been de-listed and supposedly "re-covered," twelve were actually extinct, thirty were incorrectly listed in the first place or had data errors, twelve were recovered due to actions resulting from other laws or private efforts (not the ESA), and the balance were de-listed due to management of U.S. Wildlife Refuges. The ESA has not been responsible for recovering even a single species.

The ESA costs multiple billions of dollars annually, but the land-owners who happened to have the last critical habitat needed by a species shoulder most of that cost. This is neither fair nor just when the reason the species is endangered results from the actions of society as a whole. The only solution is for federal agencies to pay just compensation to landowners adversely affected—just as the U.S. Constitution supposedly requires.

Paying for the huge costs of implementing the ESA would expose the real cost to the taxpayers footing the bill, forcing the USFWS and other agencies to prioritize what species must receive protection to allow for their recovery, while putting less emphasis on those species that are not in real jeopardy.

Imagine! The solution to finding the balance between protecting species and the landowners of America is in following the intent of the U.S. Constitution!

# DELAYING ENDANGERED SPECIES ACT PROTECTION LEADS TO EXTINCTIONS

Brian Nowicki

Congress passed the Endangered Species Act (ESA) in 1973 to provide protection to plants and animals that are in imminent danger of extinction. In this selection, conservation biologist Brian
Nowicki demonstrates that when ESA protection is not withheld
from a threatened species, that species is likely to become extinct.
Nowicki explains that when a species becomes a candidate for
ESA protection, it is placed on a candidate waiting list, where it
can stay for years before it is evaluated. Some species, such as the
Marshall's pearly mussel, are kept off the endangered species list
for what appear to be political reasons. For example, lobbyists will
fight to keep a species off the list so that construction and development projects can go forward, Nowicki reports. In many cases,
by the time protection is granted, the candidate species is already
extinct. However, Nowicki contends that when the ESA is implemented without delay, it is very successful at saving endangered
species. Nowicki works for the Center for Biological Diversity, an
organization that is advocating that all the species on the waiting
list to be immediately designated as endangered.

By 1968, it was well known that the Marshall's pearly mussel, a dis-
tinctively colored freshwater mussel that lived in the Tombigbee River
and its tributaries in Alabama and Mississippi, was highly imperiled
due to river development and engineering projects. However, in a
tragic case of political interference, the federal government did not
place the pearly mussel on the endangered species list until 1987, well
after the enactment of the Endangered Species Act that is meant to
protect species such as these—and a full seven years after the animal
had become extinct.

It is one of many animals and plants that went extinct while the
federal government delayed endangered species protections, according to a report . . . released by the Center for Biological Diversity. The

Brian Nowicki, "Delays in Endangered Species Act Protections Lead to Extinctions,"
*Earth Island Journal*, Autumn 2004. Copyright © 2004 by Earth Island Institute. Reproduced by permission.

report found that 108 animals and plants are known to have become extinct since the creation of the Endangered Species Act in 1973, including 83 plants and animals for which endangered species protections were significantly delayed.

Together, these species' stories document how the failure to implement the Endangered Species Act adequately and in a timely manner has allowed the extinction of many of these plants and animals. Some 25 of these became extinct in the first few years of the Endangered Species Act, before any protections had been implemented.

Twenty-nine others became extinct before they had been officially identified as candidates for endangered species listing, such as Florida's emerald seaslug, California's Breckenridge Mountain slender salamander, the Oregon giant earthworm, and West Virginia's Rich Mountain cave beetle.

Another 11 became extinct despite eventual listing as endangered species; due to significant delays in the listing process, the protections came too late. These include California's Fresno kangaroo rat, several species of Hawai'i's Oahu tree snails, the Mariana mallard, and the golden coqui, a Puerto Rican amphibian.

However, the majority—49 plants and animals—went extinct while the federal government delayed endangered species protections, in many cases purposefully. All of these plants and animals had been identified as imperiled, either by Fish and Wildlife Service reports or scientific petitions submitted by citizens or conservation organizations.

## Delaying ESA Protection

In many cases, the Fish and Wildlife Service identified the plants and animals as needing endangered species protections, but delayed these protections by instead placing them on the candidate list, an administrative waiting list that provides no protections and has no time limit. Many plants and animals became extinct while they remained on the candidate list or while the Fish and Wildlife Service endlessly reviewed petitions and reports.

In the case of the Marshall's pearly mussel, construction on the Tennessee-Tombigbee Waterway project—a two-billion-dollar effort by the Army Corps of Engineers to connect the Tennessee and Tombigbee rivers through 205 miles of man-made canals and locks—was set to commence in 1971 when a federal judge halted the project. The judge sided with conservation groups that asserted that the federal government had not adequately analyzed the environmental impacts of the massive river engineering—impacts that were expected to include the extinction of five native mussel species. In fact, the US Department of Interior also submitted a letter warning of the impending extinctions.

However, waterway construction began again in 1972 when a federal court ruled it was not expressly illegal to cause a species to go extinct.

The following December, the Endangered Species Act of 1973 changed that. From that day forward, the Army Corps of Engineers and all government agencies were prohibited from causing the extinction of plants and animals on the federal endangered species list. At that point, if the Fish and Wildlife Service had listed the mussels as endangered, the waterway project would have had to be redesigned in order to save them. But that is not what happened.

To avoid conflict with powerful lobbies supporting the waterway project, the Fish and Wildlife Service delayed listing the imperiled mussels for several more years while waterway construction got underway. In 1976, the Office of Endangered Species issued another warning about the likely extinction of the mussels. Two years later, Fish and Wildlife Service biologists spoke out against the delayed protections. Finally, in 1979 the US General Accounting Office issued a report exposing the politicization of the endangered species listing process, prompting the Fish and Wildlife Service to announce in 1980 that the mussels were being considered for listing as endangered species.

The government postponed the actual listing for several more years, until 1987. By then, the waterway project was well underway, and the Marshall's pearly mussel had been extinct for seven years.

## Continued Extinctions

Marshall's pearly mussel is just one of many species that went extinct while the Fish and Wildlife Service delayed endangered species protections. There are numerous other examples.

The four-angled pelea is a sprawling shrub found on the forested mountain slopes of Kauai, Hawai'i. The pelea was last seen in 1991 after waiting 16 years without protection as the Fish and Wildlife Service reviewed its petition.

The keeled sideband is a terrestrial snail found in the forests of the Sierra Nevada of California. The sideband was listed as a candidate in 1984—the last year that it was seen—after waiting 11 years for endangered species protections.

The Amak Island song sparrow is a songbird that nests in the tundra of Alaska's Aleutian Islands. The Amak Island sparrow declined for eight years while under petition, and was last seen in 1988.

An even more tragic example is the Guam broadbill, a small, blue, fly-catching bird that inhabited forests and mangrove swamps of the United States territory of Guam. The broadbill declined due to habitat destruction and predation by brown tree snakes that were introduced to the island.

The songbird had already been lost from two thirds of its habitat by the time the Endangered Species Act was enacted in 1973, but a significant population still existed and could have been saved through protection and captive breeding. However, no action was taken to protect the broadbill until the Governor of Guam petitioned the Fish and

Wildlife Service in 1979. At the same time, the governor also requested that the northern coastline be designated as critical habitat for the bird.

The Fish and Wildlife Service placed the broadbill on the candidate list, where it waited until 1983—and until the population had already declined to as few as 100 individuals in just 150 acres of forest habitat. The last Guam broadbill was seen in March 1984. The Fish and Wildlife Service listed the bird as endangered five months later—five years after the governor had petitioned to protect it.

The broadbiil is just one of many Guam species or subspecies that became extinct while the Government delayed urgently needed protections, including the Mariana fruit bat, Guam bridled white-eye, Guam cardinal honey-eater, and Guam rufous fantail.

The Center for Biological Diversity report found the highest numbers of extinctions in the United States have taken place in the Pacific islands, the western states, and the southeastern states, and almost half of all extinctions since the enactment of the Endangered Species Act have occurred in Hawai'i.

## ESA Successes

There is, however, a strong indication that when properly implemented, the Endangered Species Act has been successful at saving species from extinction. Of the more than 1,200 species in the United States that have been listed as threatened or endangered, only 23 have become extinct, and 12 of those suffered significant delays in protections. That is a success rate of over 98 percent—in so far as these species are still alive in the wild today.

Unfortunately, delays and extinctions have plagued the Fish and Wildlife Service over the entire 30 years of the Endangered Species Act. . . . The Bush administration is greatly exacerbating the problem by systematically delaying and denying endangered species listings, achieving the far lowest listing rate in the history of the Endangered Species Act. In fact, the Bush administration has so far listed only 31 species as threatened and endangered, compared to 521 under Clinton and 234 under the first Bush administration. Furthermore, the current administration has failed to list a single endangered species except in response to citizen petitions and lawsuits.

The Center for Biological Diversity has called upon the Bush administration to immediately propose endangered species listings for all 256 plants and animals currently waiting on the candidate list, and to develop a five-year plan to finalize endangered species protections for them all.

# THE SCIENTIFIC BATTLE OVER THE KLAMATH RIVER

Robert F. Service

Robert F. Service covers issues in the Pacific Northwest for the journal *Science*. In the following selection, Service writes about the disagreements between biologists over the endangered status of fish in the Klamath River. Service reports that fisheries biologists working for a range of government agencies—from the U.S. Geological Survey to the California Department of Fish and Game— insist that water levels in the Klamath are linked to the health of endangered salmon and sucker populations and that the provisions of the Endangered Species Act therefore forbid tampering with the river. However, Service relates that a panel from the National Academy of Sciences has concluded that there is no basis for these findings, meaning that the government has no justification for restricting access to irrigation water from the river. Now, Service writes, fisheries biologists on the Klamath fear that the ongoing battle over the importance of water levels may doom future efforts to protect the river's endangered fish populations.

As a cold February night settles in, Rip Shively wades into the icy waters of Upper Klamath Lake near the Oregon-California border and hauls ashore a squirming, meter-long fish. The fish, netted as it prepared to spawn, is an endangered male Lost River sucker. Shively, a fisheries biologist at the U.S. Geological Survey (USGS), scans the fish with a wand. Similar tests on about a dozen earlier catches produced no response, but this time the wand beeps, indicating that the fish had been caught previously and tagged. Based on its size, Shively judges the sucker to be more than 15 years old, and from the tag's location on the fish's back, he surmises that it was tagged in 1995. That means it lived through three massive fish die-offs that hit the lake in 1995, 1996, and 1997. "She's beautiful," he says. "A real survivor."

Shively and colleagues at USGS and other government agencies, universities, and Indian tribes are racing to study the suckers and en-

Robert F. Service, "'Combat Biology' on the Klamath," *Science*, vol. 300, April 4, 2003, p. 36. Copyright © 2003 by American Association for the Advancement of Science. Reproduced by permission.

dangered coho salmon that swim the Klamath River below the lake. Their work guides federal plans to prevent the fishes' extinction. Federal wildlife managers used the scientists' preliminary research to recommend limiting the withdrawal of irrigation water from the lake in 2001 to minimize the impact of a regional drought on the endangered fish. But a report issued [in 2002] by the National Academy of Sciences (NAS) has cast a cloud over much of the fisheries research in the Klamath Basin. The report concluded that there was "no sound scientific basis" to justify turning off the irrigation spigot from the lake to farmers dependent on its water for crops.

## Junk Science?

The report's conclusion sparked an outcry in this small farming community that federal agencies are supporting "junk science," and it bolstered calls for reforming or scrapping the Endangered Species Act (ESA). But . . . it has also sparked another, more muted outcry, this one among fisheries biologists. They contend that the report's analyses were simplistic, its conclusions overdrawn, and—perhaps worst of all—that the report has undermined the credibility of much of the science being done in the region if not fueled an outright anti-science sentiment.

"The opinions of [NAS's National Research Council] committee pretty much run counter to [those of] all the people who work in the region," claims Mike Rode, a fisheries biologist at the California Department of Fish and Game (DFG) in Mount Shasta, California. "It was very offensive to many folks here," adds Larry Dunsmoor, a research biologist working for the Klamath Tribes in Chiloquin, Oregon, who has studied the endangered suckers for the last 15 years. "It has been a very painful thing to see everything we have worked for over the past decade [described] as useless."

Biologists here are caught in a classic western water fight, one that pits two of the region's major occupations—farming and fishing—against each other. At stake is the future not just of the suckers but of the salmon downstream—and the needs of the two fish populations are sometimes also in conflict. Instead of defusing these tensions, the biologists say the report has only made matters worse, ratcheting up an already hostile environment for many of the researchers working in the area. "Some people refer to it as combat biology," says Ron Larson, a fisheries biologist at the U.S. Fish and Wildlife Service (USFWS) in Klamath Falls. "It's perhaps an exaggeration. But not by much," he says.

Now all sides are girding for another major battle, and not just over the academy's final report, which is due out [in summer 2003]. As of late March [2002] the region's snowpack was a little over half the normal level. Because snow feeds the region's streams through typically dry summers, [2002] is shaping up to be nearly as parched as 2001. [In April 2003], the U.S. Department of Reclamation is expected to make its call on how dry a summer it foresees and therefore how much lake water it expects to release for irrigation. Court rulings . . . could tighten water supplies further if judges rule that additional water must be kept in area lakes and rivers to protect endangered fish.

How these events play out could set a new precedent for how much scientific proof is needed to take action to protect endangered wildlife. The ongoing NAS review of Klamath Basin water distribution evaluates whether wildlife managers have solid evidence that the actions they take will benefit species. This standard, some researchers say, is almost impossible to apply universally and could derail other protection efforts.

## Historic Battles

A quiet, high desert landscape of sagebrush and juniper, the Klamath Basin seems dominated more by solitude than acrimony. The upper basin sits on the eastern flank of Oregon's southern Cascade Mountains and is one of North America's busiest way stations for migrating waterfowl. Before the arrival of the first white settlers in the 1820s, the basin was home to members of the Klamath, Modoc, and Snake Indians. A treaty with the U.S. government in 1864 guaranteed those tribes—by then collectively referred to as the Klamath Indians—abundant fish stocks in perpetuity. But those stocks were soon to face pressures they'd never seen before.

In 1902, Congress passed the Reclamation Act in an effort to promote settlement in the arid west. One of the effort's first undertakings was the Klamath Irrigation Project to support the establishment of farms in the basin. Its target was water flowing in and around Upper Klamath Lake, 32 kilometers long but, with an average winter depth of just 3 meters, practically a pond. Homesteaders diked and drained 16,000 hectares of marshland along the lake's northern reach. To the south, an 830-km network of canals carried lake water to hundreds of farms. Seven dams were added to lakes and streams in the region to provide additional irrigation water. In 2001, the Klamath Irrigation Project encompassed 97,000 hectares of irrigable land. In addition to the farms, water from the lake also feeds a series of wildlife refuges.

In a typical year, about 62,000 hectare-meters (500,000 acre-feet) of water is diverted from Upper Klamath Lake and surrounding waterways to irrigate nearby farms. Additional water is diverted from upstream tributaries before it reaches the lake. By the mid-1980s, the lake's fish had begun to show the stress of the annual drawdowns in water and the altered habitat. Phosphorus-rich runoff from farms and ranches prompted massive algal blooms every summer, turning the lake into a vast cauldron of pea soup. The blooms triggered wild swings in the lake's acidity level and dangerous drops in the amount of oxygen dissolved in the water.

These factors, together with chronic overfishing, caused a steady decline in the lake's two populations of suckers, the shortnose and

Lost River suckers. By 1988, both species were on the endangered species list. The Klamath River coho salmon was listed as threatened in 1997. The listings required USFWS and the National Marine Fisheries Service (NMFS) to come up with recovery plans—known as biological opinions, or "BiOps"—for the fish and specify how much irrigation water the Bureau of Reclamation was allowed to divert to Klamath Irrigation Project farmers.

In its April 2001 BiOp for the suckers, USFWS biologists stated that, for the safety of the fish, the lake should not be drained below 4140 feet (1262 meters) above sea level, just below its historic level. Meanwhile, NMFS's opinion for the oceangoing coho salmon stated that the flow of water in the lower Klamath River had to stay above a minimum of 1000 cubic feet (28 cubic meters) per second.

## Cutting Off the Water Supply

But 2001 was a bad year for water. That winter, the Cascades tallied less than half the usual snowpack. Managers at the Bureau of Reclamation were in a bind. With so little water in the system and the need to fulfill the NMFS and USFWS recommendations, they announced in April that there would be no water diversions for irrigation. The head gates of the Klamath Irrigation Project were locked.

Farmers and many others in the surrounding community revolted. That summer, they staged continual demonstrations at the head gates calling for water to be released, and they even forced open the head gates briefly in an act of defiance. Angry signs sprouted throughout the community: "Some sucker stole my water," read one common refrain. A notice at a local restaurant stated that U.S. government employees were not welcome. Hoping to stay out of the line of fire, USFWS and USGS biologists went so far as to remove the government license plates from their vehicles, a practice some still follow today.

In October 2001, after much of the fervor had died down, Interior Department Secretary Gale Norton asked NAS to determine whether the water cutoff was scientifically justified. The academy's scientific arm, the National Research Council (NRC), hastily organized a 12-member panel made up primarily of academic fisheries biologists and led by William M. Lewis Jr. of the University of Colorado, Boulder. The panel was given a deadline of 3 months to turn in a preliminary report, which was published in draft form in February 2002. The final version of the interim report appeared that September.

The NRC panel concluded that most of the recommendations in the USFWS and NMFS biological opinions were scientifically justified. But it balked at the two most important ones: the minimum water level for Upper Klamath Lake and the downstream flow for the coho. "A substantial data-collection and analytical effort by multiple agencies, tribes, and other parties has not shown a clear connection between water levels in Upper Klamath Lake and conditions that are adverse to the

welfare of the suckers," the report said. As a result, "there is presently
no sound scientific basis" for the mandated lake levels. As for the
coho, it added that there was equally little justification for increased
minimum water flows down the main stem of the Klamath River.

Opponents of the BiOps seized on the panel's conclusions. "A
handful of U.S. Fish and Wildlife Service bureaucrats withheld desperately needed water from farmers in the Klamath Basin last summer.
Now we find out that that decision was based on sloppy science and
apparent guesswork. . . . This latest travesty in the enforcement of the
Endangered Species Act should be one more nail in the coffin of that
broken law," said Representative James Hansen (R-UT), chair of the
House Committee on Resources.

## A New Management Plan

Congressional representatives and farmers weren't the only ones to
draw on NRC's conclusions. In February 2002, the Bureau of Reclamation came out with a revised management plan for the Klamath Irrigation Project designed to govern operations for 10 years. The bureau
recommended dropping summer water flows in the Klamath River below NMFS's recommended 1000 cubic feet per second to provide extra
water for irrigation.

After studying the proposal, NMFS biologists concluded that the bureau's plan was inadequate to protect the coho and recommended
bringing the flows back up. In the end, the agencies settled on dropping summertime flows to as little as half the minimum recommended
in the 2001 BiOp. The bureau's plan would eventually restore the flows
by establishing a "water bank" and taking land out of production: The
bureau would "lease" water from Klamath Irrigation Project farmers,
paying to keep it in the lake and streams rather than diverting it for irrigation. ([In March 2003,] the Bureau of Reclamation announced that
it would spend $4 million this year on water leases, which it estimates
will idle 5000 hectares of farmland during the summer.)

But fish-friendly critics cried foul, pointing out that flows would
drop immediately and that the plan would restore full minimum
flows only after 9 years. As if on cue, 33,000 fish went belly-up in the
lower Klamath River in September 2002—reportedly the largest fish
kill in North American history. Most of the fish were Chinook, although some were endangered coho and oceangoing steelhead trout.
According to a preliminary report from DFG, the fish died when low
water levels forced spawners into cramped quarters, spreading naturally occurring infections. If true, it would seem to validate recommendations in NMFS's 2001 BiOp. But some have questioned DFG's
objectivity, saying that its scientists blamed federal policy for the fish
die-off before their study was even begun. The NRC panel is now reviewing the causes and will include its findings in its final report.

After the fish kill, it was the environmentalists and fishers who went on the offensive against biologists for caving in to the Bureau of Reclamation. "The current federal water plan ignores science and instead relies on guesswork, wishful thinking, and voluntary measures," said Glen Spain of the Pacific Coast Federation of Fishermen's Associations in Eugene, Oregon. "This is a water plan for killing fish. Why should farmers have all the water they need while coastal fishing-dependent communities and fishing families wind up with dead fish and dry rivers?"

In late September 2002, a coalition of fisheries groups, environmental organizations, and Representative Mike Thompson (D-CA) filed suit, seeking an injunction against the NMFS BiOp that accepted reduced flows for 9 years and asking a judge to require higher summer water flows in the lower Klamath. . . .

Bureau of Reclamation spokesperson Jeff McCracken defends his agency's handling of the water distribution plan. He says the bureau took its lead from the NRC report, which he calls "the best available science."

## The Best Science

But many fisheries biologists in the Klamath Basin disagree. "To see [the NRC report] held up as some great science proving the ESA has run amok hit us the wrong way," says Douglas Markle, a fisheries biologist at Oregon State University (OSU) in Corvallis, who co-wrote an extended critique of the NRC interim report in the March 2003 issue of *Fisheries.*

For Upper Klamath Lake, the NRC panel found that poor water quality conditions that are harmful to fish do not coincide with years with low water levels. And the best years for young fish aren't clearly associated with high water levels. As a result, panel scientists concluded that there was no clear link between lake levels and the health of fish. For the Klamath River, they found that water added in dry years to bolster flows was small "and probably insignificant." It could even make matters worse, because sun-warmed lake water might harm cold-water coho.

Few biologists claim that there is an ironclad case that higher water levels in the lake and river will always help the fish. The 2001 USFWS BiOp, they point out, didn't argue that low lake levels are always associated with poor water quality, rather that higher lake levels carry numerous benefits to water quality and fish habitat. But the NRC panel, critics charge, didn't look beyond the lack of a clear link between water levels and fish health for indications time—all other factors being equal—the fish would do better with higher water levels. The panel "pursued an unnecessarily simple view of a complex ecosystem which, combined with several clear errors in their assessment of existing data, led them to a flawed conclusion," wrote the Klamath Tribes' Dunsmoor and Jacob Kann, an aquatic ecologist at Aquatic Ecosystem

Sciences in Ashland, Oregon, in another detailed critique sent to the
NRC committee last year.

## A Complex Ecosystem

Markle and others contend that numerous examples show the importance of taking a more complex view of the Klamath ecosystem. In
the summers of 1995, 1996, and 1997, for instance, lake levels were
intermediate or high compared with the rest of the 1990s; nevertheless, the 3 years saw successive fish kills. Algae in the lake experienced
massive blooms and crashes, causing swings in pH and depleting oxygen, which can kill fish or make them more susceptible to infection.

The NRC panel noted that ". . . lake level fails to show any quantifi-
able association with extremes of dissolved oxygen or pH." But Dunsmoor and Kann argue that the panel overlooked another important
factor: wind. It aerates and mixes the water, driving much of the algae
below the level of light penetration and reducing their growth rate.
Without the wind, as in the relatively calm summers of 1995 to 1997,
the water stagnates, the algae explode, and water quality plummets.
Wind of course can't be predicted. But higher water levels, they argue,
can soften the blow by diluting nutrients to slow the algae bloom.

In 1991 something of the reverse happened. The population of
young suckers boomed, despite a lake level at its lowest since 1950.
But Markle and Cooperman note that in June, one of the most important months for the emergent fish fry, the lake level was fairly high
and dropped considerably only in October. As well, the OSU authors
point out that 1991 was a cool, windy year, which forestalled the algae bloom and led to relatively good water quality. That information
was ignored by the NRC panel, say Dunsmoor and Kann.

In a rebuttal to the Markle and Cooperman article in the same issue
of *Fisheries*, NRC panel chair Lewis fires back that "variations of
weather conditions from year to year do seem to underlie variations in
mass mortality of adult suckers from year to year, but there is no hint
of any connection with water level." And even though the notion that
a higher water level could benefit the lake fish is a plausible theory and
potential justification for keeping more water in the lake, he points
out that it's a decision based not on scientific evidence but on professional judgment. The panel, he noted, "unanimously reached several
strong conclusions because it was confident that the evidence presented to it supported those conclusions."

The scientific brawling isn't limited to the suckers. Critics charge
the committee with oversimplifying matters with regard to river-based
coho as well. The NMFS 2001 BiOp recommended releasing additional
water from Upper Klamath Lake in the summer months, in part to increase the amount of habitat available to the juvenile coho before they
migrate to the ocean. But the NRC panel concluded that additional
water sent down the main stem of the Klamath River would likely

have little impact on the tributaries where the coho linger.

The panel concluded that coho use the main stem of the river chiefly to migrate to and from the ocean. But DFG's Rode points out that some of the fish feed in the main stem for part of the day and return to the cooler tributaries while building strength for their migration. Excess water—and the habitat improvement it would bring—is of critical importance to the young fish, he says. Proponents of low river flows have used the NRC report to "try to use science to justify the low flows," Rode says.

Lewis responds that the NRC panel's job was simply to see whether flow rates were justified by documented science. "That doesn't preclude the agencies from recommending [higher flow rates] anyway," he says.

## Asking Too Much?

Perhaps the most fundamental objection to the NRC's interim report is that the panel was asked the wrong question. The committee's charge, settled upon after negotiations with its sponsors, the Departments of Interior and Commerce, was to determine whether there was scientific proof that the policies embraced by USFWS and NMFS would accomplish what they set out to do. But critics note that this isn't the standard set for the wildlife agencies. In carrying out the ESA, USFWS and NMFS are charged with using the best available science to protect the species. Where the science is questionable, they are supposed to err on the side of conservation to protect species already on the brink. In some cases, that means taking steps to preserve habitat or living conditions even if the steps haven't been proven to work.

Farmers, Markle points out, can tell you precisely how they will use a given volume of water and its value for their crops. "But with fish data, there is no certainty of the benefit you get from an added acre-foot of water or the cost of removing it," he says. By asking for scientific proof that those actions would benefit fish, the NRC panel was setting the bar too high, he says.

The trouble, adds Dunsmoor, is that the NRC report has put pressure on agencies to mandate only those recovery actions that are scientifically well established. In essence, Dunsmoor says, that puts the burden of proof on the conservation agency to show that particular management actions will help the fish: "It's a paradigm shift. It would reset how these decisions are made." To prove that a particular action will have consequences, agencies would be forced to wait until they see that harm is done by not carrying out the action, which some would say is exactly what happened with the fish kill in the lower Klamath. "All conservation goes out the window if you have to wait for fish to die to say there is an effect," Dunsmoor says.

In his *Fisheries* rebuttal, Lewis readily agrees that the NRC panel's purpose was different from that of the agencies. But he writes, "Where the economic stakes are high . . . it is useful for all parties to recognize which components of Biological Opinions are indeed scientifically solid and which are to varying degrees based on informed speculation."

## Requiring More Proof

Raising the bar on how much proof wildlife agencies must have before they take action would doom long-term restoration efforts, says Mark Buettner, a fisheries biologist at the Bureau of Reclamation. One example, he says, is the ongoing effort to prevent phosphorus-rich farm and ranch runoff from reaching Upper Klamath Lake. Even if vast strides are made in reducing the amount of phosphorus that reaches the lake, such an effort may not have an impact on water quality for years or decades to come. That's because the lake's muddy bottom is chock-full of phosphorus and other nutrients that leach back into the water, Buettner points out. If wildlife agencies were required to show a rapid effect of their actions, reducing nutrient inflows—which virtually all fisheries experts agree is important—would never get off the ground.

It may take decades of research to demonstrate any link between lake level and the health of the endangered fish. But many researchers worry that public reaction to the NRC interim report could undermine the research efforts needed to unravel the basin's complex ecology. "It has led many nonscientists to the conclusion that the question [of proper management] has been answered," Larson says. "It's frustrating," says one biologist who asked not to be identified. "What we do has instantly become junk science." The NRC panel may soften its tone in the final report. But many on biology's front lines here fear that the damage has already been done.

# THE ENDANGERED SPECIES ACT IS THREATENING FARMERS AND RANCHERS ON THE KLAMATH RIVER

William F. Jasper

William F. Jasper is senior editor for the *New American*, a biweekly newsmagazine that is dedicated to exploring current issues from a conservative point of view. In the following selection, he discusses the conflict between farmers, ranchers, environmentalists, and the federal government over use of water from the Klamath River on the Oregon-California border. Some of these interested parties want to allocate the river's water for irrigation; others believe the draining of the water will threaten endangered fish in the river. In 2001, Jasper explains, the government, at the request of environmental groups who cited the Endangered Species Act (ESA), refused to release any water for irrigation, contending that the fish would be critically harmed by low water levels. However, Jasper contends, the government's decision was based on faulty, fraudulent science. He argues that the ESA is being used as a weapon by environmentalists to completely prevent farming, ranching, and logging operations on the Klamath River and elsewhere, not to protect endangered species. Jasper insists that the government should put human needs first, and must abolish the ESA.

Menacing storm clouds have been hovering over the Upper Klamath Basin on the Oregon-California border [since 2001]. Unfortunately, they are not the kind of clouds that bring rain, which would be most welcome in this beautiful, but arid, high plateau on the eastern slope of the Cascade Range. These dark clouds have produced only political thunder and lightning in a heated struggle between the area's farming/ranching community and federal agencies allied with environmental activists.

In the dry lands of the Western states, there is an old saying:

William F. Jasper, "Water Is for Fighting," *The New American*, vol. 20, August 9, 2004, p. 10. Copyright © 2004 by American Opinion Publishing Incorporated. Reproduced by permission.

"Whisky is for drinking, water is for fighting!" And nowhere is the fight over water more intense than in the Klamath Basin. On July 17, [2004], five U.S. congressmen representing California and Oregon districts held a special hearing in Klamath Falls, Oregon, on the impact of the Endangered Species Act (ESA) on rural communities throughout the West. Farmers, scientists and public officials testified concerning the destructive effects of ESA policies on people as well as animals and the environment. Hundreds of area residents turned out at a prehearing rally that symbolized the frustration felt by millions of Americans who are feeling the brunt of the federal environmental hammer.

## Conflict on the Klamath

Although the ingredients for the present conflict had been brewing for years, even decades, the shot that started things was fired by the federal government on April 6, 2001. On that date, the U.S. Bureau of Reclamation (BOR) decreed that area farmers and ranchers would not be allowed to use any of their allotted irrigation water. "April 6, 2001 has been etched in the minds of people in these parts as another 'Day of Infamy,' like Pearl Harbor, December 7, 1941," Professor Ken Rykbost, an hydrology expert and critic of the federal policy, told *The New American*.

The federal government cited the Endangered Species Act (ESA) as justification for cutting off the farmers' water in the critical planting season. The farmers' water had to be taken, said the BOR, for the benefit of the Lost River sucker and the short-nose sucker, both of which had been listed as "endangered" in the Upper Klamath Lake, and the coho salmon, which was listed as "threatened" in the Klamath River. This meant, said the BOR, that Upper Klamath Lake must be kept at historic high levels for the sucker fish and that more water had to be released into the Klamath River for the coho—ergo, water for the fishies, not for the farmers.

The rich, volcanic soil of the Klamath Basin is excellent agricultural land, but the area averages only 13–15 inches of rain per year. Irrigation is essential to growing crops in this region, and surface water from Upper Klamath Lake and the Klamath River is the main irrigation source. Cutting off access to water is the equivalent of sounding a death knell for area farms.

Many of the roughly 1,500 farmers who cultivate the Klamath Basin are veterans or descendents of war veterans, who were lured to the area as homesteaders following World Wars I and II. Along with the deeds to their land, they received deeded water rights, guaranteeing allotments of water for each growing season, "in perpetuity." The April 2001 cutoff was unprecedented. It was also economically devastating to the entire region, not just to the farmers directly affected.

When the cutoff occurred, many farmers had already spent or borrowed thousands or tens of thousands of dollars for seed, fertilizer, fuel and labor for that year's growing season. Many already had contracts to deliver their crops. Some of those who had already planted were forced to let their crops parch in the sun; some were able to irrigate with well water—at a much higher price that wiped out most, if not all, profit. Cattle were auctioned off at distressed prices. Many family farms were forced into bankruptcy, and many of the farmers who have managed to hang on are still hovering close to the financial edge.

Greg Williams, a banker with Northwest Farm Credit Services in Klamath Falls, Oregon, told *The New American* that the cost to the area for the 2001 water shut-off is estimated to be around $200 million. Many of the region's farmers calculate the cost at several times that amount and have brought a suit against the federal government for $1 billion in damages.

## The Federal Government's Fish Story

Adding salt to the farmers' wounds is the knowledge that the ostensible reason for their woes—the supposedly endangered species—is merely a pretext for a broader agenda based on radical environmental ideology and quack "science." The 2001 BOR decision to refuse water to the farmers was based on two "biological opinions"—one issued by the U.S. Fish and Wildlife Service for the sucker fish and the other by the National Marine Fisheries Service for the ocean-going coho salmon. It was soon revealed that the biological opinions that were endangering the survival of many family farms had not been subjected to outside peer review and were badly flawed in many important respects.

In response to the uproar caused by the federal water policy, the National Research Council (NRC), the operating arm of the National Academy of Sciences (NAS), established a special committee of scientists to investigate the matter. On March 13, 2002, Dr. William M. Lewis, chairman of the NRC/NAS committee, testified before the Resources Committee of the U.S. House of Representatives. Dr. Lewis, professor of Environmental Science and Director of the Center for Limnology at the University of Colorado, reported that the NRC/NAS consensus contradicted the opinions undergirding the government's draconian water policies.

"Despite the availability of a substantial amount of data collected by federal scientists and others, no clear connection has been documented between low water level in Upper Klamath Lake and conditions that are adverse to the welfare to the suckers," the professor told the congressional audience. "For example," Lewis stated, "incidents of adult mortality (fish kills) have not been associated with years of low water level. Extremes of chemical conditions considered threatening to the welfare of the fish have not coincided with years of low water level, and the highest recorded recruitment of new individuals into the population occurred through reproduction in a year of low water level." Thus, said Lewis, the NAS scientists found "no sound scientific basis" for the federal policies ordering arbitrarily high lake levels and shutting off the irrigation valves.

The NRC/NAS study confirmed what many other scientists had already been saying about the so-called science providing the foundation for the new Klamath water policies. Among the many facts that are seldom, if ever, reported in the major media are these important points:

- There is no scientific "consensus" that the "endangered" sucker fish are truly endangered.
- Evidence shows that both species of sucker fish thrive with shallower, warmer lake levels, not with the historic high water levels recommended by the federal agencies.
- Putting more of the warm Klamath Lake waters into the Klamath River instead of into irrigation not only hurts the farmers but the coho salmon, which need colder water.
- The Upper Klamath Lake area provides only 3.4 percent of the water flow at the mouth of the Klamath River and would not provide a much higher percentage even if all of the Upper Klamath waters were diverted to the river.
- Diverting more of the irrigation water to "wetlands" will hasten the dehydration of the area and could cause much of the Upper Klamath Lake and Klamath River to dry up completely in drought years.
- The seven years chosen as the basis for the government's biological opinion were some of the wettest years on record in the past century, with 34 percent higher than normal inflows to the Upper Klamath Lake and 21 percent higher precipitation. Using these wet years as the norm radically skewed the BOR's lake level recommendations to the ultra-high end.

In short, fedgov's fish story is a whopper.

## Weapon for the Green Agenda

Like Americans in many other parts of the country who have been victimized by edicts and rulings under the Endangered Species Act, the overwhelming majority of Klamath Basin residents are thoroughly convinced the ESA is being used as a weapon against people—and specifically against the farmers—rather than as a remedy to help the fish. And, for once, even the ultra-liberal, ultra-green *New York Times* has voiced agreement.

In a June 24, 2001 piece on the Klamath imbroglio, entitled "An Endangered Act: Sacrifices to a Green Agenda," *Times* writer Douglas Jehl noted that "much of the trouble the act has prompted comes from lawsuits brought by environmentalists who have learned to use the Endangered Species Act as a weapon." Mr. Jehl, in a moment of candor rare for the *Times*, explained further:

Cast in the name of plants and animals, these lawsuits tend to have humans very much in mind. In their fights against logging, shopping malls, housing tracts and the like, environmentalists have found that they can erect no better barrier than persuading the Fish and Wildlife Service that the land is home to an endangered species. And they enlarge that obstacle by arguing that its home stretches far and wide.

That is precisely the pattern followed by the eco-fanatics in the actions that have brought about the . . . Klamath crisis. The federal decision to pull the plug on the farmers stems from ESA lawsuits brought by the Oregon Natural Resource Council, the Arizona-based Center for Biological Diversity, and the Earthjustice Legal Defense Fund (formerly Sierra Club Legal Defense Fund).

Many officials and scientists in the federal agencies resist the environmental radicals and try to administer the laws fairly and reasonably. But, over the years, a sizeable cadre of eco-extremists has grown within many of the agencies. For them, like their professional activist brethren in the Big Green organizations—Greenpeace, Environmental Defense, World Wildlife Fund, Sierra Club—the ESA is sacrosanct, trumping the U.S. Constitution, the Ten Commandments, the laws of nature, property fights and common decency. For them, it is, as *Timesman* Douglas Jehl pointed out, a weapon—a political weapon of mass destruction.

## Fishy Science

In June 2001, shortly after the government turned off the Klamath irrigation spigots, biologist David A. Vogel blasted that policy decision before the House Resource Committee field hearing in Klamath Falls. Mr. Vogel, a fisheries scientist with 29 years' professional experience, including 15 years with the U.S. Fish and Wildlife Service and the National Marine Fisheries Service, declared that the Klamath farm situation is an "artificially created regulatory crisis that has been imposed on the Upper Klamath basin" without any semblance of sound science.

"In my entire professional career," Vogel said, "I have never been involved in a decision-making process that was as closed, segregated, and poor as we now have in the Klamath Basin. The constructive science-based processes I have been involved in elsewhere have involved an honest and open dialogue among people having scientific expertise. Hypotheses are developed, then rigorously tested against empirical evidence. None of those elements of good science characterize the decision-making process for the Klamath Project."

Vogel charged that the U.S. Fish and Wildlife Service "so selectively reported the available information that it can only be considered a distorted view of information available to the agency at that time." The government's own USFWS surveys, he pointed out, found both species of sucker fish to be "relatively abundant." In short, listing the suckers as endangered was rotten science, if not outright fraud.

## Exposing Fraud

This was not the first time government biologists had resorted to fraud; in some cases, their conduct has gone beyond unethical into the criminal realm. Such was the case, for instance, regarding the planting of Canadian lynx hair in forests in Washington State to stop logging and recreational activities. Forest Service officials also were caught spreading seeds of ESA-listed plants in the San Bernardino Forest to stop mining operations and knowingly using false data concerning spotted owl habitat to stop timber harvests in California.

In 2002, the National Association of Home Builders scored a major coup in exposing the fraudulent "science" employed by the National Marine Fisheries Service in designating more than 150 watersheds in California, Oregon, Washington and Idaho as critical habitat for salmon and steelhead. In a lawsuit challenging those watershed designations, the builders association produced a "smoking gun" internal memo by a high-level government official admitting to bogus methodology. "When we make critical habitat designations," said the memo, "we just designate everything as critical, without an analysis of how much habitat" is actually needed for salmon populations.

When government officials with these attitudes work in tandem with the professional radicals from environmentalist groups, as they regularly do, the results are devastating. More than 500 animal species and over 700 plant species are listed under the ESA as "endangered" or "threatened." Dozens more plant and animal species have been officially proposed for listing and hundreds more species are official candidates for listing. Hundreds of "habitat conservation plans" affecting millions of acres have been mandated. These ESA mandates regularly place absurd restrictions on human activity in every state of the union for the alleged benefit of dung beetles, snail darters, minnows, sand flies, spiders, spotted owls, mice, toads, snakes and other feathery, furry and scaly critters.

The ESA listings are used to stop or severely restrict farming, grazing, logging, brush trimming, fire fighting, manufacturing, mining, hunting, fishing, hiking, camping, rafting, boating, snowmobiling, four-wheeling and many other activities. They are used to stop the building of barns, homes, hospitals, schools, factories, parks, golf courses and many other projects.

## Lethal Policies

The fanatical zeal of the militant enviros and government bureaucrats can even prove deadly for humans. That's what happened on July 10, 2001, when four fire fighters trapped in the "Thirty Mile Fire" in Washington's Okanogan National Forest were sacrifice to the supposed benefit of the endangered bull trout. The stranded fire fighters radioed for helicopter water drops and waited in vain for more than nine hours, before they were killed by the blaze. Meanwhile, Forest Service officials dithered, worried that dipping the helicopter buckets into the nearby river might violate the habitat of the bull trout.

The Klamath Basin policies may not have caused any human deaths thus far, but it is arguably the largest and most severe assault on a single area. The Klamath Basin area directly affected encompasses the city of Klamath Falls (20,000 population) and the smaller Oregon towns of Merrill, Keno, Malin and Midland, as well as the California border communities of Tulelake, Hatfield and Tuber.

Not long ago the Klamath Falls area had a robust wood products industry base. But in the 1980s and 1990s, the Fremont and Winema National Forests were largely closed to logging, thanks to the ESA and the spotted owl. Bill Ransom, a Klamath Falls farmer, also worked many years in the timber business. "People around here see the same thing happening to the farming base that happened to our timber industry," he told *The New American*. "Most of the mills around here have been closed down. The same government agencies and environmentalists are now trying to use the same kinds of arguments and fake science to destroy farming in the area."

Despite the NRC/NAS findings and other . . . developments favoring Klamath farmers and discrediting the government's water policies, the federal agencies continue to use the discredited biological opinions to mandate water levels that deny farmers most of their irrigation water. Prior to 2001, area farmers could count on 350,000 to 400,000 acre/feet of water for the area's 200,000 to 220,000 acres of crops—mostly potatoes, onions, cereal grains, mint and alfalfa. In 2001, the water was cut off completely, then turned back on to a bare trickle in July, after it was too late for most crops. Since then, the farmers have been forced to give up 75,000 acre/feet of water per year, ostensibly to help the fish and area wetlands. In 2005, the water they must yield up increases to 100,000 acre/feet.

## Glimmers of Hope

"Constantly losing more and more of our water is bad enough," says Bill Ransom, "but the real problem is that you just live under the constant fear that they could come in like in 2001 and do it again, just cut off all the water, at any time, right in the middle of growing season, and destroy everything, without any rational basis, without any peer-reviewed science—just by a simple, bureaucratic mandate. That's not right and that's what we're fighting."

[In 2004] the Ninth Circuit Court of Appeals, generally recognized as the most radical federal court in the land, surprised most observers by ruling against the federal government's listing of Oregon Coastal coho salmon as threatened. The Ninth Circuit let stand an earlier ruling by U.S. District Court Judge Michael Hogan that the National Marine Fisheries Service must count hatchery coho along with "wild" coho. The reason: According to the DNA evidence and the scientific consensus, the two fish populations are indistinguishable from one another, swim side by side in the rivers and streams, and have been spawning together for the past century. The illegal counting method used by the agency's "scientists" allowed them to obtain a false low fish count to justify listing the coho as threatened, as well as to justify draconian land use and water use policies.

However, the litigants and their supporters, who had fought for so long to reverse the coho salmon's "threatened" designation, may have little to celebrate. On May 28, [2004,] the Bush administration stunned many observers when it announced new proposals by NMFS to leave in place 26 ESA listings for Pacific salmon and steelhead populations, despite the rulings by Judge Hogan and the Ninth Circuit and the steadily mounting scientific evidence that many of these fish populations are not at risk.

Now the ball is in Congress' court; it created the Endangered Species Act and has allowed its massive, unconstitutional abuses. It's time now for Congress to send the ESA to extinction.

# LIVING WITH THE ENDANGERED SPECIES ACT

Dave Wortman

In this selection, freelance author Dave Wortman discusses how the Endangered Species Act (ESA) has affected life on the Puget Sound in Washington state. In 1999, the government qualified wild chinook salmon populations in the sound for endangered species protection. Although residents were fearful of lawsuits and economic troubles stemming from the endangered designation, Wortman writes that the region came together to help protect the species, which is considered an icon of local life. However, deciding how best to protect the chinook has not been easy, the author continues. Moreover, some business leaders think regulations protecting salmon go too far in protecting the fish at the expense of human needs. Wortman reports that continuing growth in the region means that community leaders will have to plan for how to mitigate the impact of human development on the chinook. Wortman works for the Seattle-based development planning group Adolfson Associates, which specializes in environmental consulting.

On a summer day in 1999, Pat Cagney, a biologist with the U.S. Army Corps of Engineers, stood on the banks of Washington's Skagit River surveying the nearby shores of Puget Sound. The dike running under his feet held fast against the river's swirling waters—waters that once fanned out across a broad estuary, creating complex braids of fresh and salt water and a refuge for young salmon on their journey to the sea. Now, the dike forced both river and salmon to head downstream.

On the dike opposite Cagney, a crowd of politicians and reporters anxiously stood by, and soldiers from Fort Lewis dug holes and set the final charges. A series of muffled explosions ripped through the dike. For the first time in nearly 60 years, two miles of river were set free to roam across the once adjacent estuary. River and sea would soon meet again. Cagney and others hoped that the salmon would follow.

"This is the kind of project we need to give young salmon a real

Dave Wortman, "Can Cities and Salmon Co-Exist?" *Planning*, vol. 68, May 2002. Copyright © 2002 by American Planning Association. Reproduced by permission.

chance for survival," he said in a recent interview.

The Skagit River's Deepwater Slough Restoration Project is just one of dozens aimed at restoring the Puget Sound region's devastated wild salmon runs. . . . March [2002] marked the third anniversary of a milestone for the salmon. In 1999, the National Marine Fisheries Service, the federal agency with authority over "anadromous," or ocean-going salmon, declared the sound's wild chinook population one of several salmon runs along the West Coast threatened or in danger of extinction.

The listing triggered widespread fears of economic disaster and lawsuits. In response, the region has spent millions of dollars restoring habitat, studying salmon biology, and assessing the impacts of urban development. But a major question remains: How will the salmon's listing ultimately affect the region's way of life? With Washington State's population projected to double in the next 50 years, the answer is still far from clear.

## An Icon

Living with species on the edge of extinction is nothing new to the Pacific Northwest. The fierce controversy over the northern spotted owl sent shock waves through its timber industry in the early 1990s. But for salmon, an icon in the Pacific Northwest, it's a different story.

For one thing, salmon migrate hundreds of miles from ocean to mountain streams. Thus, the endangered species listing affects farmers, loggers, fishermen, rural landowners, and urban residents, virtually all of whom live within the watersheds of Puget Sound. To many, a Northwest without salmon is like a forest without trees.

"As far as the impacts of the Endangered Species Act on a human population, this is simply unprecedented," says Curt Smitch, Washington Gov. Gary Locke's top advisor on salmon issues.

Chinook salmon, also called "king," is the largest of the Pacific salmon, commonly reaching three feet in length and weighing more than 30 pounds. In late summer and fall, adults lumber up the region's rivers to spawn. Tiny juveniles emerge in the spring, guided downstream on currents of fresh snowmelt.

Like most salmon, chinook thrive in cool, clean streams with deep pools and forested banks. But returning salmon now face channelized streams, banks stripped of vegetation, impassible culverts, and urban runoff. Populations of wild chinook have declined sharply in the last 30 years.

On the Cedar River east of Seattle, the number of chinook returning to spawn dropped to just a few hundred in the mid-1990s. In some watersheds, wild chinook have all but vanished.

## A Region Comes Together

The chinook's 1999 listing came as little surprise to Puget Sound's elected officials. For years, leaders watched as surging growth and faltering salmon runs put the region on a collision course with the Endangered Species Act.

"I think the writing was on the wall at that point," says Bruce Laing, Fellow of the American Institute of Certified Planners (FAICP), a former King County council member who is coordinating the region's salmon recovery efforts. "It really became a matter of how we would respond."

In February 1998, the impending listing brought together 35 leaders from the region's three most populous counties—King, Pierce, and Snohomish—to discuss the salmon's fate. The gathering included county executives, mayors, tribal leaders, and environmental groups. "Many areas of the country might see the listing as an infringement, but here we saw it as an opportunity," says Laing. "Salmon are a symbol of our quality of life, so we asked the question, what can we do about it?"

Answers did not come easily. Complex factors affect the wild chinook's health: stream and river habitat, hatchery programs, ocean harvest, climate, and dam operations.

"Discussions of the causes of this decline often seem like sort of a lunatic firing squad in which people form a circle and shoot at whoever's across from them," says Jim Lichatowich, one of the Pacific Northwest's leading fish biologists.

Over the next 18 months, the self-labeled Tri-County coalition, along with staff biologists and consultants, worked with the National Marine Fisheries Service to explore the causes of the chinook's predicament. The coalition members researched how far to set back development from salmon streams, how to control stormwater runoff, and how to improve road maintenance practices.

Initially, Tri-County sought coverage under section 4(d) of the Endangered Species Act, which allows certain land development activities and government operations to be shielded from legal challenge. But when the fisheries service released its final set of 4(d) rules for the chinook in July 2000, the TriCounty's plans to protect the fish were not included.

"We've learned a lot in two years," says Meg Moorehead, coordinator of Snohomish County's Endangered Species Act response program. "There is still hope, but also a more realistic notion of what can be done."

Tri-County has completed its own biological review of its proposal, which includes wider vegetative buffers along salmon streams, more storage for stormwater runoff, and stricter clearing and grading standards. Over the long term, the coalition anticipates spending millions on land acquisition and habitat restoration. But, asks Laing, "how much funding is the public willing to support? At this point, we don't know the answer."

While elected officials and planners search for answers for the salmon listing, landowners face uncertainty, changing development standards, costly studies, and project delays. Many projects requiring a federal permit or approval, from large road projects to housing developments, have come to a standstill.

Bonnie Shorin, a biologist with the National Marine Fisheries Service, says that Section 7 of the Endangered Species Act requires federal agencies to assess the impacts on the chinook of every federally funded or permitted project, from wetland permits to transportation funding. "We're literally looking at thousands of projects a year," she says, noting that Washington State's staff of 30 reviewers has been overwhelmed, creating project delays of up to a year.

Building industry leaders think the regulations protecting salmon go too far. "The irony is that these sweeping regulatory changes won't make any difference in the recovery of salmon but will effectively squeeze thousands of families out of the housing market," says Tom McCabe, executive vice-president of the Building Industry Association of Washington. His group is seeking to de-list the chinook, citing . . . [an] Oregon court decision that hatchery and wild salmon should be treated equally in listing decisions.

Jay Johnson, senior project manager of the Bentall Corporation, a real estate company based in Vancouver, British Columbia, has first-hand knowledge of practices in Washington State. At first glance, his company's Millennium Office Park seems typical of new developments in the region's high-tech landscape. Six modern office buildings spill across a 30-acre site in Redmond, a fast-growing Seattle suburb.

In fact, Millennium is atypical. In 1999, just before the chinook's listing, Johnson's company approached Redmond for a development permit and was met with a long list of requirements to protect and restore salmon habitat in nearby Bear Creek. The company agreed to set aside more than 20 percent of the site in stream buffers, place logs in the stream, and plant native streamside vegetation at a cost of more than $3.5 million.

"No one will argue that some restoration isn't good, but it's the extent that is the question," says Johnson, noting that he now considers the city's requirements as a taking of property. Still, Johnson cannot deny that salmon are spawning in the company's restored section of stream.

Considering the region's continuing growth, a major shift in thinking is needed if the salmon is to be saved, says biologist Jim Lichatowitch. "More than any single heroic rescue, restoring healthy runs of Puget Sound chinook will require a new philosophy toward the landscapes both we and these fish call home," he says.

There is some hope. Three years after the Skagit River dike came down, in the restored backwaters of the river's Deepwater Slough, the young salmon have returned.

# CHAPTER 3

# PROBLEMS WITH ENDANGERED SPECIES CONSERVATION

Contemporary Issues
Companion

# SHOULD PARASITIC SPECIES BE SAVED?

Matt Kaplan

In the following selection, author Matt Kaplan discusses a problem that troubles conservation biologists: how to decide which endangered species to save? In particular, Kaplan explains, scientists are concerned about organisms such as intestinal parasites that live in endangered species such as white rhinos and douc langurs. Some parasites can be critical to the survival of their host species, he writes, while others may be contributing to health problems. Many scientists stress that all organisms have the right to live, Kaplan reports, but they will not preserve parasites that are harmful to endangered animals. Biologists are attempting to tackle the problem by studying the relationship between parasites and hosts, Kaplan relates, so that they can eventually have a better understanding of whether or not harmful parasitic organisms should be saved. Kaplan writes about conservation and ecology issues for *New Scientist* magazine.

In October 1995 a white rhino, recently arrived in England from South Africa, excreted an insect larva in its dung. Concerned about what this maggot was doing inside their endangered animal, the rhino's new owners called in entomologist Martin Hall of the Natural History Museum (NHM) in London to have a look. The larva pupated, hatched and Hall identified it as an endangered parasitic fly that feeds exclusively on rhinos. With neither rhino to dine on nor mate to breed with, it was left to die—one less parasite in the world. Only Hall mourned its passing.

"Save the rhino maggot!" doesn't have much appeal as a conservation slogan. But the fact is that for every charismatic animal facing extinction there is an entire world of other species living on and inside it that may be equally endangered. From lice that suck blood at the surface and tapeworms that grow fat inside, to gut bacteria that aid digestion, almost every creature, especially in the wild, has hundreds of parasites that call it home. Many of these depend on one or two closely

Matt Kaplan, "Save the Rhino Maggot," *New Scientist*, vol. 181, March 27, 2004, p. 40. Copyright © 2004 by Reed Elsevier Business Publishing, Ltd. Reproduced by permission.

related host species for their survival: if their hosts become extinct, so do they. Yet, while the world's zoos spend vast amounts of time and money trying to save rhinos, pandas and the like, their parasites have never been considered . . . until now.

## Endangered Parasites

The breakthrough for the world's endangered parasites came [in 2003] when a genomics corporation called Diversa in San Diego, California, approached researchers at the Center for Reproduction of Endangered Species (CRES) at San Diego Zoo and Wild Animal Park with the idea of exploring microbial habitats within their rare and endangered animals. For Diversa this would be an amazing opportunity to do some bioprospecting in uncharted territory. The CRES researchers were equally keen, but for the different reasons. They could see the potential benefits of comparing the parasitic load of captive animals at the zoo with that carried by their wild counterparts. It seemed like a happy coincidence of interests that would give new insights into hidden worlds, but the project has already ruffled some feathers.

"This all started with gastrointestinal problems in our douc langurs, the most endangered primates in the world," says Mark Schrenzel, an expert in animal diseases at CRES. Douc langurs are likely to become extinct in the wild within a decade, yet they do not thrive in zoos. Wherever they are kept in captivity it is the same story: constant digestive problems and frequent episodes of vomiting and diarrhoea. The CRES researchers were desperate to find the source of the problem. They suspected that some of the microbes living in the guts of their captive langurs might be different from those that would normally be present in the wild. To discover whether they were right, they needed to analyse the microbial environment inside their primates.

## Analyzing Microbes

By a stroke of luck, it was then that Diversa contacted CRES geneticist Oliver Ryder, and it was agreed that Diversa researchers would work with the CRES to collect samples of microbial communities from endangered species at San Diego Zoo and compare them with similar samples taken from healthy individuals living in the wild. The hope was that they might be able to identify beneficial microbes that were missing from the captive animals. "This is an incredible opportunity to learn about the microbial diversity and symbiosis in and around endangered species and get a better understanding of the role played by organisms at the micro level," says Ryder. The plan is to study the parasites associated with a whole range of animals, including proboscis monkeys, tree frogs and dozens of ruminants. But the first candidate is, of course, the douc langur.

Research began in mid-November 2003, and the team reckons it will take about 18 months to analyse DNA from the gut of captive and wild douc langurs and compare the genetic sequences with those taken from known organisms. CRES then hopes to take organisms found in the healthy wild animals and reintroduce them to the animals in captivity. With a bit of luck, this should help to improve the balance of the captive animals' gut flora. And the langurs are not the only ones who stand to benefit. Eric Mathur of Diversa points to just one of the possible commercial spin-offs. "Discovering enzymes to improve animal feed is a major part of what Diversa does, and understanding the digestive fauna of the douc langurs helps us to gain a lot of insight in this area," he says.

In other species, the relationships between parasites and their hosts are often highly specific, so the chances of finding new and exotic organisms look good. "We used to think that roughly 50 per cent of the parasitic flatworms in the fish we study were species specific," says parasitologist Rod Bray, also from the NHM. But it seems even that figure may be too low. "Recent DNA work is showing that there is much more specificity than we originally thought," he says. And while he cautions against applying this finding to other creatures, he adds: "When it comes to parasites in fish, I think it is reasonable to say that practically every species has specific parasites."

## Exclusive Relationships

Research by Bray's colleagues highlights the sorts of barriers that can preserve an exclusive relationship between a parasite and its host. The tapeworm *Taenia olngojinei*, for example, only infests hyenas, even though its larvae are carried by antelopes, which are eaten by both lions and hyenas. But this particular tapeworm is not picked up by lions because it forms cysts within the pelvic girdle of the antelope, explains Arlene Jones, a parasitologist at the NHM. Hyenas are the only animals on the savannah with jaws strong enough to crunch through the bone and release the tapeworm larvae. "That's the one parasite we do understand," says Jones. But for most others, the reasons behind the exclusive relationship with a host remain a mystery.

If endangered animals also have unique parasites—and it seems a pretty safe bet that they do—the parasites' fate must be as uncertain as the fate of their hosts. And this then raises a tricky ethical question: should conservationists be as concerned about the fate of these parasites as they are about the survival of their hosts?

This has certainly not been a consideration until now, as the story of the California condor lice reveals. In the mid-1980s, with the California condor population down to 25 individuals, conservationists took the drastic step of bringing in all the remaining birds for captive breeding at San Diego Zoo and Wild Animal Park. Most birds have lice, so one of the first things the researchers did was to treat them with a pesticide dust to remove lice and other external parasites. Team leader Mike Wallace recalls only one or two birds having any lice at all and, as far as he and his team could tell, they were just "typical lice".

## Should Parasites Be Saved?

In light of what we have since learned about parasites and their hosts, that assessment seems outdated. "There are in fact no such things as 'typical lice'," says Chris Lyal, a louse specialist at the NHM, although when the California condors were captured this was not widely realised. The *Chewing Lice: World* checklist and biological overview, . . . published by the Illinois Natural History Survey, lists three species of louse as parasites of the California condor. Because two of them have been found nowhere else, they are seemingly extinct, says Lyal. It is impossible to say whether the San Diego Zoo's pesticide application actually caused their demise because, as Lyal points out, lice do not infest all of truer hosts equally. The two species in question may have become extinct long before the birds were taken into captivity, as the population of the host birds slumped. We will never know.

Thanks to the phenomenal efforts of CRES researchers, there are now more than 200 California condors, many of which are back in the wild. But can this breeding programme truly be considered a success if two other species became extinct in the process? Lyal, for one, is saddened by the loss. "What I don't understand is why the pesticide was used at all if the birds only had a few lice. They would not have been very damaging," he says. "In the future, we need to think very carefully about the cost and benefits of the treatments we give to endangered animals in captivity."

Not all parasites are as benign as a few lice, and those that pose a health risk to their host are certainly not going to be championed by conservationists. But where do you draw the line? What about Hall's endangered rhino maggot? This larva of the rhino botfly lives most of its life in the gut of its host, just as its close relative does in horses. "A standard riding horse can easily live a long and healthy life with a light infestation of maggots in its guts," says Hall. And if the infestation gets out of control it can be treated with one of the family of chemicals known as macrocyclic lactones, such as ivermectin. Hall sees no reason not to try and breed the rhino botfly in captivity inside its host. "It would be a challenge, but the reality is that these flies are really just a minor nuisance to the rhinos," he says. But he realises this is probably not going to happen because of the time and money it would take. While resources can be found to keep animals like condors and pandas around, who is going to stump up the cash to protect an insect whose larvae chew on the insides of rhinos?

If this seems like discrimination against species that humans find distasteful, conservationists disagree. "Our conservation efforts are guided by the needs of the species rather than by the popularity of the animal itself," says Sharon Dewar of San Diego Zoo. She points out that the zoo puts plenty of effort into conserving less popular species, including the Visayan warty pigs, red river hogs, bearded pigs and endangered cattle such as the lowland anoa and Javan banteng. But inevitably, finance is a factor. "We believe a tapeworm has a right to exist just as any other animal does," Schrenzel says. "But we do not have the resources to save everything. Our work here is focused on vertebrates and as a result they are prioritised." For Schrenzel and the other CRES scientists, the partnership with Diversa is a sideline, and the health of endangered animals remains the top priority. "We have no choice but to actively eradicate harmful parasites and bacteria from our captive populations," he says.

## Parasites Are Not All Bad

It would be hard to disagree, except that in many cases we don't actually know enough about the relationships between particular parasites and their hosts to say whether they are harmful, benign or even beneficial. Even deciding what is or is not a parasite may not be straightforward. "There is no unambiguous definition," says David Johnston from the NHM. When pressed, he recites: "A parasite is an organism that lives in or on another . . ." But then, he adds, that leads you straight into problems with species like the cuckoo, which lays its eggs in other birds' nests and fools them into raising its young. And what about the klepto-parasitic birds that harass other birds until they produce vomit, which they then eat? Or the species of fish where a male bites a female, fuses with her body and then extracts nutrients from her blood, donating only his sperm in return? The issue is very complicated, says Johnston. We call most disease-causing microorganisms "pathogenic," he points out. "Why don't we call harmful bacteria parasitic? What about viruses? Prions? Is there such a thing as a parasitic chemical?"

And there is a further problem: organisms can often fulfil different roles in relation to their host at different times of their lives and under different conditions. What can be a pathogen in some circumstances may be a commensal organism (doing neither harm nor good) or even a symbiont (benefiting the host) if circumstances change. "People almost immediately classify a tapeworm as a pathogen, yet in well-fed individuals many species are probably functioning more like commensals," says Johnston. "It is only when the going gets tough and food is scarce that the worm can start to exert a negative effect."

Then there's the finding that inflammatory bowel disease (IBD) is rare in countries where intestinal nematode worm infections are common. In a study published [in 2003,] Steve Collins and colleagues at McMaster University in Ontario, Canada, suggest that the worms themselves may play a protective role by inducing an immunological response that essentially distracts the immune system from the inflammatory responses associated with IBD.

If the relationship between organisms is so complex, has CRES set itself an impossible task in its search for douc langur symbionts? "I don't think so," says Schrenzel. "While we say that we are looking for symbionts and avoiding pathogens, we know that in reality things will not be a simple matter of black and white." The researchers believe that they have no choice but to try, given this particular primate's closeness to extinction.

But even if the beneficial gut bacteria prove elusive, the collaboration between CRES and Diversa could lead to far-reaching changes in the way conservationists think. Each endangered animal may come to be seen as an ecosystem in its own right, home to a large community of parasites that live on and in it. "Ecosystems are such complex things," says Bray. "Remove something from the system and inevitably there will be some effect. This is true of herbivores, carnivores, scavengers and even parasites."

This way of thinking makes conservation an even more difficult balancing act than it already is. But it may also offer new opportunities for the survival of animals like the douc langur. And perhaps even for some of the parasites themselves.

# INTERBREEDING CAN HARM ENDANGERED SPECIES

Donald A. Levin

Donald A. Levin is a professor of integrative biology at the University of Texas, Austin, and the associate editor of the journal *Evolutionary Ecology*. In this selection, he warns of the danger that is posed to endangered species by interbreeding and hybridization. Levin explains that, while most organisms cannot breed outside their own species—for example, because of separate habitats or different breeding seasons—when similar species are brought into contact with each other, they can sometimes mate. The result, Levin continues, is that rare species give birth to offspring that contain genes from other species. This process can dilute the genetic purity of the endangered species—and ultimately, accelerate its extinction by completely replacing the pure species with genetic hybrids. Levin stresses that conservation scientists need to be aware of the threat posed by interbreeding, and take steps to ensure that endangered species are not exposed to the risks of hybridization.

The world is awash in biological diversity. Yet even the least discerning observer will notice that the diversity of life is not a random sampling of all possible biological characteristics. You cannot find, say, organisms that are half sunflowers and half camels. Rather, nature blends only specific sets of traits, each tailored to enhance survival and reproduction. Other combinations are conceivable, but, like the sunflower-camel, they generally make no biological sense.

The well-defined sets of attributes one finds populating the natural world make up the fundamental units of bio-diversity: species. Investigations have now described nearly two million species (millions more await attention) and placed them within an elaborate taxonomic hierarchy. But even the naturalists of antiquity realized that some organisms resemble one another so much that they ought to be classified in the same general group or genus. Only much later did

Donald A. Levin, "Hybridization and Extinction," *American Scientist*, vol. 90, May 2002, p. 254. Copyright © 2002 by Sigma Xi, The Scientific Research Society, Inc. Reproduced by permission.

Charles Darwin and Alfred Russell Wallace realize that species within the same genus share many traits because they evolved from a common ancestor. That is, what was once one type of plant or animal split into two or more species.

Despite their overall similarity, different species in the same genera do not normally interbreed. They may be prevented from doing so because they have widely separated home ranges or different reproductive seasons. Indeed, that they do not freely exchange genes, for whatever reason, defines them as separate species. Yet in some circumstances separate species will mate, and if such a liaison is successful, a hybrid results.

Although such hybridization never takes place in the vast majority of genera, it is quite common in some. Botanists believe that hybridization between species happens in 6 to 16 percent of plant genera. Crossing between species is less common in animals, although it is not infrequent in some groups. For example, 9 percent of all bird species hybridize. Such a blurring of taxonomic lines also takes place within primate genera, including lemurs, gibbons and baboons. Anthropologists have even speculated that humans and Neanderthals may have once interbred.

With hybridization so rampant, one wonders how species ever maintain their distinctness. They do, in part, because the production of hybrids does not necessarily shift genetic material between species. For genes to traffic in this way, hybrids must cross with at least one of the parent species. In many instances that just doesn't happen. Why? As Darwin had observed, most hybrids are inferior to their parents: Some abort as embryos, others die as juveniles, and others still grow to adulthood but cannot reproduce. (Mules, for example, are vigorous but sterile: If you want to produce a mule, as people have been doing for more than 2,000 years, you have to mate a female horse and a male donkey. Getting it backward will result in a hinny, which is also sterile but less robust.) Hence many hybrids are unable to pass their genes back to members of their parent species.

That hybrids can survive at all is a reflection of the similarity between the parents. That they are usually weak and sterile is a reflection of the differences of the parents, whose two sets of genes were really not meant to work together. Hybridizing two species is like building a car with half GM and half Chrysler parts. It should be no great wonder that the product might not function so well.

Only in the mid-20th century did biologists recognize that, under some circumstances, hybrids can be superior to their parents. This realization stems from work of Edgar Anderson of the Missouri Botanical Garden in St. Louis, who believed that disturbance to habitat sometimes creates new conditions that are more suitable for hybrids than for the parents. He carried his argument one step further in his book *Introgressive Hybridization*, published in 1949, where he contended that, in areas of disturbance, fertile hybrids allow genes of one of the parent species to pass into the other. This process, which he dubbed introgression, could transform the species receiving the new genes enough to survive the environmental disruption.

Other botanists were slowly swayed over to Anderson's view and soon realized that habitats appropriate for hybrids—indeed where the hybrids outshine their parents—sometimes arise independently of any disturbance. In his 1997 book *Natural Hybridization and Evolution*, Michael Arnold of the University of Georgia provides a comprehensive analysis of this phenomenon. There he details the adaptive advantage of hybrids in habitats where environmental conditions are intermediate between those of the two parent species. Biologists are aware of many such places, which often contain multiple types of hybrids (termed hybrid swarms) in addition to the parent species. Sometimes the hybrids constitute a majority, and crosses between them and one or both of the parents mongrelizes the pure species, that is, takes away their genetic distinctiveness. One yardstick of mongrelization is what the organisms look like, but easily observable traits are sometimes misleading. Hence biologists frequently choose to examine telltale genetic markers, which show clearly whether the species under investigation has been "infected" with alien genes. Such work has . . . uncovered, for example, that introgressive hybridization has been blending two species of Atlantic redfish off the coast of Newfoundland.

## The End of the Line

Although hybridization and the enhanced adaptability it provides is sometimes beneficial, it can also be detrimental, because it allows an abundant species to drive a rare relative to extinction. John Harper, a plant ecologist at University College in North Wales, first recognized this possibility in 1961. The actual threat of hybridization to some species became apparent during the 1970s, as investigators studied more rare species and began applying the tools of molecular biology.

It is easy to see why certain organisms are at risk. Rare species often flourish only because they are isolated from related ones and therefore cannot cross with them. As Phillip Levin and I pointed out . . . , modern civilization is carving up natural habitats, separating like organisms in a way that might ultimately foster speciation for some groups of plants and animals. But people's activities are also eroding physical and ecological barriers, allowing once-isolated species to make contact locally or even over large regions. In Louisiana, for example, farmers' pastures and irrigation ditches brought distinct species of Iris together over wide areas. Herbert Riley of the University of Kentucky and Anderson studied the resultant hybrid swarms more than 50 years ago.

Similar changes to the natural environment have spurred the hybridization of animals. For example, the alteration of water courses for flood control and irrigation affords easy avenues for the intermingling of certain aquatic species. Or consider the settlers who planted trees on the Great Plains during the 19th century. They inadvertently provided stepping stones for the westward expansion—and subsequent hybridization—of several species of birds, including grosbeaks and jays. In the Northeast, people's meddling with the environment has led to hybridization between golden-winged and blue-winged warbles and between the American black duck and mallards.

Indeed, mallards have been spreading their genes far and wide. Brought to Hawaii in the early 1900s as game birds, they have been mating with the Hawaiian duck. And since being introduced to New Zealand in the 1930s, European mallards have been hybridizing with the native grey ducks there. Although it is not impossible for a species to hop over geographical or ecological barriers on its own and land in the neighborhood of a relative, such jumps seldom happen naturally. Even an Olympic-class mallard, for example, would be hard pressed to make it across the Pacific. But since the time of Columbus (and even before), people have routinely transported plants and animals—either purposefully or accidentally—all over the globe.

Not surprisingly, hundreds of different organisms brought from distant continents have escaped and crossed with indigenous species. That process affects, for example, the plant *Lantana depressa*, which is endemic to Dade County, Florida. There *L. depressa* is hybridizing with the introduced *L. camara*, a species common in southern gardens. The hybrids, which combine the local adaptations of the native and vigor of the alien, have thrived and are spreading.

## Elbowing Out the Cousins

The proliferation of an exotic species need not in itself spell trouble for native species, but it often does. One problem is reproductive interference: when the introduced organism leads to failed matings (ones that produce no progeny) or matings that yield only hybrids. One illustrative example of this process involves female European minks, which can mate with their kind as well as with introduced American minks. After linking up with their Yankee cousins, the Europeans are averse to mating with males of their own species. Accordingly, the number of European minks born in areas where these two species are in contact is much reduced from normal levels. For the tsetse fly and certain bird parasites, reproductive interference is even more dramatic. The very act of mating with a different species results in the death of the females through a mechanical incompatibility between genitalia.

Even when the failure to mate is not a major issue, the process of hybridization itself can threaten a species simply because it leads to fewer pure progeny. If the parents of a particular species have, on average, just one pure offspring each, the population will just be able to

84                                                    ENDANGERED SPECIES

maintain its numbers over time. Hybridization can then tip the balance, so that each organism produces less than one pure offspring. When this happens, the population declines in size. The fewer the number of pure offspring, the faster the slide to extinction.

Simple arithmetic explains why when two species hybridize, the less abundant one usually suffers the most: All else being equal, the minority species sustains a proportionally greater decline in its reproductive rate. Harlan Lewis, a botanist from the University of California, Los Angeles, showed how this mechanism worked in artificial mixtures of the annual plants *Clarkia biloba* and *Clarkia lingulata*, where the former outnumbered the later by a ratio of five to two. These species cross readily, and their hybrids are sterile. To no one's surprise, in Lewis's experiment *C. lingulata* was hybridized out of existence through the loss of reproductive capacity. These results bear directly on wild *C. lingulata*, which is known only from two sites in the Sierra Nevada of California, one of which is separated by only 100 meters from a population of *C. biloba*. The continued existence of *C. lingulata* is clearly in jeopardy.

A rare plant or animal can be driven to extinction even when the hybrids are not sterile. The abundant relative just overwhelms it. That is, the fertile hybrids provide pipelines for the movement of genes from the abundant species into the rare one, contaminating its gene pool. Soon all of the rare organisms are tainted with alien genes, and eventually the rare species no longer exists as such. It is first mongrelized, then fully assimilated.

The Catalina Island mountain mahogany, *Cercocarpus traskiae*, provides an illustrative example of this process. This species, California's rarest tree, is confined to a single canyon on Santa Catalina Island, which lies roughly 60 kilometers off the coast of southern California. The 40 mature trees noted when this species was first described in 1897 have now dwindled to 12 adult plants and some 75 seedlings. The principal cause of this precipitous decline is clear: The sheep, cattle and other animals brought to the island over the past 150 years have grazed on too many of the seedlings. This tree also suffered from hybridization with the birch-leaf mountain mahogany, *Cercocarpus betuloides*, which is more abundant on the island. In 1996, Loren Rieseberg and Daniel Gerber of Indiana University showed that nearly half of the adults and some seedlings of *C. traskiae* contain alien genes. Assimilation seems likely unless drastic steps are taken.

Another prime example of this phenomenon involves a plant named *Argyranthemum coronopifolium* (a relative of chrysanthemum), which is restricted to the Tenerife, one of the Canary Islands. This plant has been found at only seven sites, three of which are in various stages of hybridization with its more prolific cousin, *A. frutescens*. Roads built in the past 50 years hastened the spread of *A. frutescens* to the restricted habitats of *A. coronopifolium*. At one site, contact first took place in 1965. By 1985 only a few pure examples of the rare daisy remained, and they were embedded in a hybrid swarm. Now there are only hybrids and the invading *A. frutescens*. At another site on the island, the beleaguered species has been reduced to a few individuals, now far outnumbered by the hybrids and attackers. Similar encounters with *A. frutescens* also threaten the survival of two other species of *Argyranthemum* on Tenerife.

Such assaults on rare plants are not uncommon. As Judy Rhymer of the University of Maine and Daniel Simberloff of the University of Tennessee pointed out a few years ago, some of the plant species on the Nature Conservancy's vulnerable list are apparently at risk because they are hybridizing with numerically superior relatives. Included on that tally is the white fire-wheel (*Gaillardia aestivalis*) of Texas, which is hybridizing with the Indian blanket (*Gaillardia pulchella*), a flower the Texas Department of Transportation likes to plant along roadways. Also, the last population of the Bakersfield saltbush (*Atriplex tularensis*) seems to be mongrelized by the widespread *A. serena* in Kern Lake Preserve of California. Similarly, the California sycamore (*Platanus racemosa*), which grows along the Sacramento River and its tributaries, is being amalgamated with the London plane tree, and the California black walnut may have been infused with genes of several other walnuts. Oddly enough, the London plane tree is itself a hybrid of the oriental plane (*Platanus orientalis*) and the American sycamore (*Platanus occidentalis*), and was imported from Europe.

In each of these cases, a rare species suffers at the hands of a more abundant relative, but this imbalance is not a prerequisite. For example, on the shores of San Francisco Bay, the native California cordgrass (*Spartina foliosa*) is hybridizing with smooth cordgrass (*S. alternifolia*), which was introduced in the 1970s. Despite its small numbers, the exotic species is at an advantage because it produces 21 times as much pollen as the native. Moreover, the pollen of smooth cordgrass is superior: Some 23 percent of the flowers will set seed with it, whereas only about 4 percent will do so with pollen of the native. As a result, San Francisco Bay has a large population of hybrids, which are spreading at the expense of the native and may ultimately replace it.

This type of exposure to introduced plants is particularly strong when crops are grown in the vicinity of rare wild relatives. Even if only a tiny fraction of the pollen from the sown fields reaches the native plants, significant hybridization can result. As Normal Ellstrand of the University of California, Riverside, and his associates recently noted, 12 of the world's 13 most important food crops hybridize with wild relatives in some part of their ranges. These include wheat, rice, maize, soybeans and barley. Sometimes this process endangers the wild stock, as is the case for Hawaiian cotton and some African rices. In most other situations, when the wild type is relatively common, the species is not put at risk. The reason is simple: When crop genes infiltrate a natural population, they are not apt to spread far, because they are typically detrimental. But this generalization need not hold in all cases.

One of the best studied exceptions is with sunflowers. Domesticated and wild varieties of the common sunflower (*Helianthus annuus*) grow side by side in many locations. Honeybees pollinate both types, and the two interbreed readily, producing fertile hybrids. Randal Linder, one of my departmental colleagues, and his coworkers analyzed the extent to which three populations of wild sunflowers shifted their genetic makeup in the direction of a domestic variety growing nearby in much larger numbers. The wild populations and domesticates he investigated have been in contact for between 20 and 40 years. In that time, the genetic constitution of the wild plants shifted about 35 percent in the direction of the cultivated variety.

The danger domesticates pose for their wild cousins is even more evident for some animals. Consider our greatest friend, the dog. All members of the dog genus, *Canis*, can, in principle, interbreed and produce fertile offspring. So the potential for gene swapping between domesticates and wild relatives is quite real. Indeed, the work of Carles Vila and Robert Wayne of the University of California, Los Angeles, suggest that dogs and wolves (*Canis lupus*) have exchanged genes repeatedly since domestication began, some tens of thousands of years ago (if not longer). Hence most taxonomists now reward dogs and wolves as members of the same species.

The most threatened canid is the Ethiopian wolf, which is known from fewer than 500 individuals in six small isolated populations. Hunting and destruction of their natural habitat have devastated these animals. Wild dogs now outnumber them by 10 to 1. Genetic studies by Vila, Wayne and their colleagues revealed that from 8 to 17 percent of the wolves in one of the six groups are of hybrid ancestry, the result of matings between female wolves and male dogs. (Because females normally leave their pack to copulate with male wolves from neighboring territories, they often encounter dogs and mate with them.)

The housecat (*Felis catus*) is another domesticated culprit polluting the gene pools of wild animals. Like the dog, this species has in many parts of the world established feral populations, which can interbreed with their local relatives. In Europe, for instance, hybridization between wild and domestic cats is pervasive. Such interbreeding is thought to be the least prevalent in northern and western Scotland; yet even there approximately 80 percent of the the wildcats (*F. silvestris*) show genetic markers that are characteristic of their domesticated cousins.

## Solving the Problem

Environmentalists have focused considerable attention on protecting rare species from the destruction of their habitat and from hunting and predation, as well as from the disease and outright competition for resources they often face when encountering introduced species of a like kind. Clearly, hybridization needs to be added to this list of threats.

Preservationists should recognize that what some endangered species need most is to be isolated from their close relatives, whether indigenous or introduced. This measure is simple enough to take in some settings, for example, in botanical gardens. Yet even at these bastions of conservation, I have been surprised to find collections of rare plants growing within pollination range of their close relatives. Another way to save rare plants and animals is to remove pure individuals from threatened populations and relocate them to a place where related species are absent.

But what do you do if an organism is on the verge of extinction, when only a few individuals are left anywhere? Do you breed it with a relative with the hope of salvaging some of its distinctive characteristics, or do you let it expire? You would probably choose to breed it, because, after all, something is better than nothing. So if only a handful of survivors remain, or if they are all of one gender, then hybridization with a relative is the only logical course of action. But what should your strategy be if, say, 30 or 40 individuals remain in the wild?

This very situation confronted those struggling to save the Florida panther, *Felis concolor coryi*, a subspecies of cougar (or, equivalently, puma). Restricted to south Florida, one of the two largest groups lives in the Everglades; the other inhabits Big Cypress Swamp. Although it has been protected from hunting for more than three decades, the Florida panther remains in decline, in part because of reduced male fertility. Indeed, these panthers have the worst sperm observed in any amimal: About 95 percent of their sperm cells are malformed. Also, the incidence of cryptorchidism, a defect that causes one or both testicles to remain undescended, has risen from negligible levels to 80 percent since 1980. To make matters worse, these panthers have enormous parasite loads, which cause debilitating disease or even death.

The plight of the Florida panther stems in part from its low level of genetic variation, a direct result of its small numbers and the inbreeding that has gone on. To address this genetic impoverishment, conservation managers hatched a plan in 1992 to introduce the Texas puma (*Felis concolor stanleyana*) into Florida. Although this step compromises the Florida panther's very identity as a distinct subspecies, the experts concluded that the animal's critical status demands it. They decided that the Texas puma was a good source of new genes because the two cats formerly had overlapping ranges and probably once interbred in the wild.

Thus far this program appears a success. Crosses between the two types of cats have resulted in a few dozen progeny, and some of those hybrids have themselves procreated. So the number of panthers in Florida is on the upswing.

This experience suggests that forced cross-breeding is an excellent strategy, at least when closely related subspecies can be paired up. But the value of this approach becomes less clear if the endangered animal must be bred with an entirely different species. In that case, even specialists may be challenged to determine the biological compatibility between the species and to judge the vigor of their progeny. What is more, crossbreeding separate species muddies the legal waters and may dilute the safeguards afforded to the animal under the Endangered Species Act. As it stands, the U.S. Fish and Wildlife Service has no established policy for hybrids, and because the Act defines only vaguely what species warrant protection, hybridization truly complicates matters.

Another problem—for both biologists and lawyers—is that one doesn't always know whether an endangered species is pure. Consider the red wolf of the southeastern U.S. In the late 1970s, ecologists noted that the count of red wolves was frighteningly low and that these animals were increasingly interbreeding with coyotes. Responding to this crisis, scientists found a small number of "pure" red wolves and started a captive breeding program to save the animals from extinction. More than a decade later, Wayne and Susan Jenks of Sage College in Albany, New York, scrutinized DNA evidence and uncovered that the red wolf wasn't a distinct species at all. Rather, it appears to be a hybrid—part coyote, part gray wolf.

In light of these findings, should the government have spent millions of dollars protecting the red wolf? And should the programs continue? Wayne believes that they should, because preserving the red wolf could maintain characteristics no longer found in nature. (The original red wolf may have come from a match between a coyote and a now-extinct subspecies of gray wolf.)

Others might argue that "contaminated" species should not have government protection, but the question remains on the table. Hybridization should be promoted when it is necessary to maintain deteriorating populations, and it should be prevented when it threatens rare species. Thankfully, people are becoming increasingly aware of these problems. For example, the Hawaiian duck's race toward extinction prompted both U.S. and international agencies to address the problem of its hybridization. In 1992, the Rio convention of biological diversity discussed the dangers of hybridization and the safeguards that need to be put in place before an exotic species is released into a new environment. And in 1999 an executive order of President Bill Clinton created the National Invasive Species Council expressly to deal with such issues. These are good first steps, but as I have tried to show here, conservationists must think about hybridization between native species, too.

# THE ENDANGERED SPECIES TRADE: PROHIBITION VERSUS SUSTAINABLE USE

Rolf Hogan

In the following selection, freelance journalist Rolf Hogan reveals the dilemmas that surround efforts to protect endangered
species from illegal trade. The Convention on International
Trade in Endangered Species (CITES) limits or bans trade in certain endangered animal products, such as ivory, Hogan writes.
However, he continues, some conservationists believe that allowing sustainable use of some endangered species—for example,
the selling of rhino horn from existing stockpiles—may be a key
to saving them. The white rhino is one species that has benefited
from an emphasis on sustainable use, Hogan reports. Revenue
from ivory sales and hunting permits has provided money to
prevent poaching and protect white rhino habitat. Despite the
white rhino success story, however, opponents believe that limited sales of endangered animal products will encourage more illegal trade and poaching of endangered species, the author finds.
Moreover, restrictions on trade encourage wildlife smugglers to
become more sophisticated. Hogan concludes that the wildlife
trade can provide protection for some endangered species, but it
may push others closer to extinction.

South Africa [has] announced that it is ready to part with 1,500 elephants which, it says, are destroying trees that other species depend
on for their survival in the country's famous Kruger National Park. If
there are no takers the animals will be culled and their tusks added to
South Africa's bulging ivory stockpile.

The South African offer highlights a critical dilemma facing all
those concerned with wildlife conservation: is it possible to protect
endangered species like elephants and rhinoceros effectively if trade
in wildlife products, even on a one-off basis, is allowed? South Africa

Rolf Hogan, "The Wildlife Trade: Poacher or Gamekeeper," *UNESCO Courier*, July
2000, p. 12. Copyright © 2000 by the United Nations Education, Scientific and Cultural Organization. Reproduced by permission.

is one of many African countries which argue that a limited trade in wildlife product stockpiles should be allowed so that the proceeds can be used to pay for conservation. Governments and conservation groups that are hostile to this approach claim that any kind of sale will stimulate the illegal market, encourage more poaching and ultimately push species such as elephants and rhino closer to extinction.

## A Controversial Issue

The debate on this controversial issue reaches a crescendo every two or three years at the Conference of the Parties to the Convention on International Trade in Endangered Species (CITES). The convention has 151 member states which vote at the conference on proposals to limit or place an outright ban on international trade in species considered to be at risk. At the CITES conference held in Nairobi, Kenya, in April [2000], calls to lift the ban on trade in products such as ivory, turtle shells and whales provoked fierce debate.

While countries like Kenya and India opposed lifting the ban on the ivory trade, Japan and Norway wanted the ban on whaling lifted because, they said, the stocks of some whales on the endangered list are healthy enough to withstand commercial harvesting. After long deliberations, the CITES parties agreed to maintain the existing trade ban on ivory products, turtle shells and whale meat [until 2003].

Conservationists no longer oppose the idea of wildlife being exploited per se. If properly managed, they say, wildlife can provide food for impoverished rural populations and wildlife-based tourism can be an important source of income.

However, the sustainable use of wildlife means striking a delicate balance. "We only support using wildlife where it is beneficial to both the local community and to the ecosystem," says Gordon Sheppard of the World Wildlife Fund (WWF).

"It is oversimplistic to ban trade," says Jon Hutton, director of Africa Resources Trust (ART), an NGO involved in community conservation schemes in southern Africa. "We need to assess the trade-offs and come to a rational decision. We have to weigh up the profits from trade that can be reinvested in wildlife conservation, through funding government law enforcement or indirectly through providing an income for local communities, against the possible costs, such as an increased risk of poaching.

"In much of Africa, wildlife represents a net cost. It can kill people and damage crops and is therefore eradicated, either deliberately or gradually by exclusion. More and more land is being converted to agriculture, even if it is marginal for livestock, because rural people often have no alternative. ART is involved in schemes which return wildlife ownership to farmers. They then have a choice between cattle and crops or wildlife, and in many cases, they choose the second. Wildlife can be sold three times: to tourists, to sport hunters, and finally as ivory and hides. The sale of wildlife products often brings in the most revenue. The sale of ivory and hides for example represents 80 per cent of the value of an elephant. Tourism can bring in revenue, but most of the profits are made by international tour operators and not by local communities. Sport hunting on the other hand can bring in enormous revenue for the local community and it can be carried out in areas that may not be suited to tourism."

While the "non-consumptive use" of species for tourism is accepted by most wildlife organizations, some are against "consumptive use"—the killing of animals for food or profit. Animal welfare organizations believe that it is almost impossible to exploit animals without severely affecting their populations. "In principle, it is a nice idea," says Sarah Tyack of the International Fund for Animal Welfare (IFAW), "but there are too many examples of where it has failed."

## Rhino Revenue

In practice, experts say managing sustainable use of a species can be very difficult because wildlife needs and animal behaviour patterns have to be carefully balanced with human needs. Some species such as the hawksbill turtle, can easily be overexploited, and uncontrolled tourism can severely affect some species. In Kenya's famed Masai Mara reserve, for example, scientists found that the hunting success of lions was reduced by a heavy inflow of tourists. Large groups of tourist vans tend to gather around the cats and frighten off their prey. "The key to using wildlife sustainably is good management but in many countries the resources or expertise are simply not available," says Sheppard.

South Africa provides a good example of the sustainable use of an endangered species.

The African white rhinoceros is one of the most endangered animals on earth but South Africa, as home to 80 per cent of the estimated 8,500 animals remaining in the wild, has plenty. Well protected from poaching, South Africa's rhino population is growing. "Numbers could double in a decade," says the World Conservation Union's (IUCN) Rhino Specialist Group, "but only if there is sufficient new land for surplus animals."

The South African government argues that if it were allowed to export rhino horn, currently banned under the CITES, the revenue generated would help to pay for rhino conservation. What is more, profits from rhino horn would act as an incentive for private landholders and communities to maintain wild areas for rhino conservation.

South Africa charges a trophy fee for rhino hunting, which generated $24 million between 1968 and 1996, when the country's white rhino population quadrupled. Revenue from hunting finances the high cost of protecting rhinos from poachers, which can be as much as $1,000 per km$^2$ per year.

The interest in rhino has also helped fund national parks. When protected from poaching, rhino populations can increase to a level where they are too numerous to survive in limited park areas. To keep populations within ecological limits, live rhino are sold to private rhino sanctuaries. In KwaZulu-Natal, sales of live rhino, which can fetch up to $30,000 per head, generated a turnover of $1.57 million in 1998, and [1999's] rhino sales provided about 10 per cent of the KwaZulu-Natal Nature Conservation Service's operating budget. "In a time of declining government spending on conservation," says Martin Brooks, head of Scientific Services with KwaZulu-Natal Nature Conservation Service, "wildlife sales have been a vital source of revenue for conservation."

## Encouraging Illegal Trade

However, other African states, which do not have sufficient funds or staff to tackle poaching, argue that any legal trade in rhino horn will stimulate the illegal market and lead to heavy poaching.

For example, people living in Damaraland in northwest Namibia are against lifting the ban on trade in rhinos. When the region's rhino population was dwindling in the early 1990s due to illegal poaching, the Save the Rhino Trust, a UN-sponsored group, started a project which encouraged local populations to benefit from rhino through ecotourism. The project has been successful in generating revenue for the local community, and former poachers have even been recruited as rhino trackers for tourists.

"We worked with the communities and they saw that the rhino were worth more to them alive than dead," says Simon Pope, who worked on the project. "The people worked hard to save their rhino but were very worried about international trade in rhino horn being allowed. They believed that it would encourage poachers to come and take away their livelihood." Unprotected by park rangers, rhinos on communal lands would be especially vulnerable to increased poaching.

Japan, which strongly opposed boosting trade restrictions at the [2000] CITES conference, argued that complete protection of endangered species would be detrimental to national economies and communities dependent on wild species for their livelihoods. During the conference, Japan and Norway aggressively lobbied for removal of the Minke and Grey whales from the endangered species list.

It is estimated that there are more than a million Minke whales. Japan and Norway argue that the population is healthy enough to allow a sustainable harvest. However, many conservationists insist that the other great whale species have not yet recovered from centuries of commercial slaughter and that a limited trade in Minke whale meat could not be regulated well enough to prevent the illegal hunting and sale of meat from these protected species.

What hard evidence exists to show that limited trade in wildlife products might stimulate consumer demand and lead to increased poaching? In 1997, the CITES conference sanctioned the one-off sale of ivory stockpiles from Africa to Japan as an experiment. About 60 tonnes of ivory were sold. Two years later African governments, including Kenya, and a number of international conservation organizations quoting independent studies, argued that poaching and the movement of illegal ivory stocks had increased as a result of this one-off sale.

There are nevertheless questions about whether trends in poaching and the illegal market can be inferred from studies which, due to paucity of funds, are often weak in their methodology and focus on limited areas. "Independent studies from non-governmental organizations can be unreliable," says Sabri Zain of TRAFFIC, an international organization set up by the IUCN and WWF to monitor international trade in wildlife. To help to fill this gap, the European Union has promised to donate four million Euros ($4 million) to monitor elephant poaching and the illegal trade in ivory.

Another key problem is that of enforcing international trade bans and keeping tabs on regulated sales. "Tiger poaching for bones for traditional Chinese medicine, as well as for skins, remains a grave threat," says Peter Jackson, chair of the IUCN's Cat Specialist Group. "Unfortunately effective measures to control or reduce illegal trade are seldom enforced in most range countries, despite resolutions by the CITES Conference of the Parties."

Advocates of trade argue that tighter controls simply incite smugglers to become more sophisticated and drive illegal trade further underground. Furthermore, some wildlife derivatives are almost impossible to detect. Raw ivory might be difficult to conceal but tiger bone can be powdered and rolled into cigarettes or boiled down into gelatine.

Meanwhile, conservationists have been active in curtailing demand for some wildlife products. Education programmes in China have encouraged consumers to reject tiger bone remedies and an international campaign is currently underway to highlight the plight of the Tibetan antelope, which is in danger of being hunted to extinction for its fine fur, used to make highly sought after shahtoosh shawls.

Conservationists have also co-operated with Chinese medicinal practitioners to find alternatives to tiger bone and rhino horn, which are used in traditional medicines. Mole rat bone is now being promoted in China as an alternative to tiger bone and there is some evidence of a reduction in the use of tiger-based medicines. Less than five per cent of Asian consumers surveyed in Hong Kong, Japan and the United States said that they had actually used medicine containing tiger parts.

## Declining Resources for Conservation

Trade bans should probably be given more time to see if they can be made more effective through international pressure on governments and educating consumers. "A trade ban can only be as effective as the national measures taken to stop illegal hunting and trade, and the efforts made to enlist the involvement of governments and consumers," says Steven Broad, director of TRAFFIC.

But some argue that trade or no trade, time is running out for wildlife. "The biggest single threat to wildlife is the destruction of habitat," says Simon Rietbergen of IUCN. The figures are alarming: we have already removed or seriously degraded 80 per cent of the planet's forest cover and 50 per cent of the world's wetlands. "Lack of resources and declining government budgets for conservation are leaving many parks without adequate protection," says Rietbergen. No matter how effective a trade ban, it cannot slow down the current rate of habitat loss or pay for wildlife protection. Trade which has the potential to save more wild areas and pay for their protection may ultimately be the preferred option.

# HABITAT PROTECTION THAT MAY DO MORE HARM THAN GOOD

Joni Praded

Joni Praded writes about wildlife and environmental issues for magazines such as *Animals* and *E.* In this selection, she reveals that an Endangered Species Act (ESA) amendment that is meant to preserve habitat for endangered species may actually be harming the organisms it is meant to protect. Praded explains that landowners can circumvent ESA requirements by developing habitat conservation plans (HCPs) that set aside land for endangered species. While this idea was initially lauded by environmentalists, Praded writes, in practice it has allowed developers to clear huge tracts of land, while only saving tiny parcels for the endangered organisms. In addition, she relates, conservationists believe the HCP process is not properly handled. They point out that permits often allow construction to occur in areas with endangered species, meaning that habitat that should be protected is put at risk. Ultimately, Praded concludes, HCPs may do more harm to endangered species than good.

On a cool California morning, all is quiet at Crystal Cove State Park. Hillsides flanked with rare coastal sage scrub lead down to an expanse of empty beach. In this Orange County outpost, just three joggers pass by in half an hour, while shorebirds skim the waves and a dolphin breaks the horizon in the nearby surf.

Amid the hubbub of fast-growing southern California, this place could seem astonishingly serene. But it doesn't take long to spot the real action. Just across the Pacific Coast Highway, which rims the park, undulating hills mark the massive holdings of the region's largest private landowner, the Irvine Company—and bulldozers churn their way through scrub to clear the land for single-family homes on some of the nation's most valuable real estate. It is real estate coveted by endangered species and humans alike. The process that took this parcel from wildland to housing lots is billed by some as conservation-friendly

Joni Praded, "The Real-Estate Crunch," *Animals*, vol. 133, September 2000, p. 14. Copyright © 2000 by the Massachusetts Society for the Prevention of Cruelty to Animals. Reproduced by permission.

smart growth, and by others as the nation's endangered-species policy gone awry.

The Crystal Cove area is not alone in its transition. All over southern California, construction crews are transforming rare, unspoiled wildlife habitat into housing or commercial spaces. It surprises many to learn that this part of California—home to L.A. smog and Hollywood hype—is one of the most biodiverse regions of the continental United States. With its extensive variety of habitats, it supports a wide array of plant and animal species—many of them found nowhere else on earth. In fact, one-fifth of all species on the federal endangered list are found in California. So, too, are 36 million people, and southern California's population is expected to grow by 6 million—or two Chicagos—over the next 20 years.

## Circumventing the Endangered Species Act

Before the early 1990's such development was frequently stalled by endangered or threatened creatures that most had never heard of before. Corporate and private landowners became entangled in lengthy permit battles as they sought to circumvent the stringent requirements of the Endangered Species Act (ESA), which would have prevented them from altering their land in any way that would add to the risk faced by troubled species.

The region eventually became the ground for bitter battles as species such as the coastal California gnatcatcher and the Stephens' kangaroo rat threatened to halt big-ticket development plans. The federal government, weary from the spotted-owl wars in the Pacific Northwest, looked anywhere it could for compromise and found it in a little-used 1982 amendment to the ESA. This amendment allowed landowners to receive permits to harm or kill endangered species in exchange for developing habitat conservation plans (HCPs) on their property. Despite its drawbacks, many U.S. Fish and Wildlife Service (USFWS) officials say that the HCP approach, while far from perfect, is better than its alternative—reviewing each permit application individually. Says USFWS Assistant Field Supervisor Jim Bartel, "The project-by-project method is not efficient and is limited in its ability to address a lot of species and a lot of habitats. If your preserves are all postage-stamp preserves, many species are going to be doomed."

At the time, many environmentalists lauded the move, believing, for a while, the HCP promise of a winning outcome for everyone, including endangered critters. But today, with 270 HCPs covering 20 million acres of land in the country, conservationists and scientists are analyzing what has been gained and what has been lost. And, they say, the picture is not always rosy.

Take the case of the coastal California gnatcatcher, a diminutive, grayish blue songbird with a home range limited to coastal southern California and northwestern Baja California, Mexico. It lives almost exclusively in coastal sage scrub, where it thrives on insects and, in breeding season, fashions grasses, bark strips, small leaves, spider webs, down, and other materials into nests that rest just three feet above the ground.

When the USFWS responded to petitions to list the species as endangered in 1993, estimates cited between 1,800 and 2,500 pairs in their highly fragmented southern California habitat. Worse, the gnatcatcher lived mostly on private property, including land owned by several major companies.

For years battle lines were etched in the scrub over the listing. In 1991, when the USFWS announced its intention to designate the bird as endangered, it received two petitions—one containing 9,000 signatures supporting an emergency listing, another with 6,000 signatures opposing it. Predictably, conservation groups and scientific organizations were among the supporters; labor and building industry organizations joined a number of landowners in opposition.

If the gnatcatcher were listed, development could have been barred on every acre the species occupied until, and unless, developers received "incidental-take permits." These permits, costly and time-consuming to obtain, are essentially ESA exemptions granted on a project-by-project basis to individuals or companies that agree to minimize their impact and compensate for any habitat they intend to disturb—usually by setting aside or restoring suitable habitat elsewhere.

Meanwhile, a state harboring some of the nation's most expensive real estate and anticipating substantial population and economic growth had been looking for a way to merge the disparate interests of the land-rights and conservation communities. The state legislature passed the Natural Community Conservation Planning Act of 1991 (NCCP)—a measure that aims to provide for regional biodiversity protection "while allowing compatible and appropriate development and growth." Unlike the ESA, the NCCP focuses on crafting conservation agreements that cover many species and many landowners over a long period of time. And unlike the ESA, it is voluntary.

## Reaching a Compromise

The small songbird that had become the country's most noted casualty of urban sprawl became the NCCP's pilot project, and planning to create protected areas got under way. But according to a Natural Resources Defense Council (NRDC) report, relatively few acres were in fact enrolled in conservation plans, and development on unenrolled lands continued full-force: "In Orange and San Diego counties alone, over 7,600 acres of coastal sage scrub were razed during the program's inaugural years, hardly a mark off the preceding period"—with most of the clearing done where the gnatcatcher usually nests.

Fearing a spotted-owl-like standoff and responding to a property-rights lobby that was already calling for Congress to weaken the ESA,

Secretary of the Interior Bruce Babbitt responded with something that would characterize his tenure: compromise. The bird was listed in 1993, but as threatened, not as endangered. And with the listing came a special rule that allowed the recovery efforts to be managed by California's NCCP process—similar to the HCP process.

A grand experiment ensued, and it influenced the handling of all subsequent endangered-species issues. But warns NRDC senior attorney Joel Reynolds, "The truth is, we're not going to know if it's a success or failure in a true sense for 100 years or more."

What the HCP and the NCCP processes boil down to, say Reynolds and others, is a leap of faith. And it's a leap made much more frightening by a "no-surprises" clause that was added to HCP language in 1994 to further appease the concerns of private landowners. Essentially, the clause assures anyone entering into an HCP-type agreement that no additional funds or land will be required of them even if situations change drastically or plans fail—except in extraordinary circumstances.

"These no-surprises clauses have been implemented in more than 250 conservation plans since the administration came in," reports Leona Klippstein, conservation programs director for the southern California-based Spirit of the Sage Council. According to Klippstein, "Back when the HCP amendment was made, there was a big problem with the environmental groups in Washington not understanding its potential. What it essentially did was gut the Endangered Species Act.". . .

## Inadequate Measures

A federal judge [has] declared several high-profile HCPs in Alabama illegal. The case involved the critically endangered Alabama beach mouse. The USFWS had issued incidental-take permits for large-scale beachfront developments that would destroy the little occupied habitat the erosion-controlling mouse still maintains.

Environmental attorney Eric Glitzenstein comments, "The HCPs approved by the USFWS relied on 'mitigation' measures that ranged from the truly laughable—including the placement of signs warning young children that they should stay off sand dunes occupied by endangered mice—to the patently inadequate—such as meager cash payments for 'offsite mitigation,' which, the record showed, would not be sufficient to purchase even a fraction of the amount of habitat obliterated by the projects."

Glitzenstein, Klippstein, and several other environmentalists and scientists say that HCPs like the one for the Alabama beach mouse are all too typical. "You hear 'habitat conservation plan' and it sounds very good," says Klippstein. "But the sole purpose is [to allow landowners] to get an exemption from the ESA and kill endangered species. Why make exceptions? Why make it voluntary? They did not need habitat conservation plans, and they did not need the State of

California's NCCP program." If Klippstein's Spirit of the Sage Council has its way, both these programs will be rescinded. The group, joined by several other national conservation groups, has a lawsuit pending against the Interior Department, challenging the legality of the administration's no-surprises rule.

The no-surprises rule, they say, departs significantly from the way other environmental or public-protection laws are implemented. Glitzenstein explains it with a comparison: "When the Environmental Protection Agency issues permits for the discharge of emissions into the water and air, or for the storage of hazardous wastes—which would otherwise be unlawful under the Clean Water Act—it does not give dischargers an additional 'incentive' to comply with these laws by promising them that their permit conditions will never change even if the permitted activities turn out to be far more detrimental to the public health and environment than previously believed."

## Problems with Habitat Conservation Plans

Reviews of existing HCPs have pointed to a host of shortfalls, from lack of public input to lack of sound science in the planning process. A 1999 study found that 30 percent of HCPs allow 100 percent of endangered species to be eliminated in their permit areas. In response to these and other criticisms, the USFWS and the National Marine Fisheries Service issued a policy to toughen HCP requirements in five areas; this includes establishing better biological goals and objectives, managing for inevitable changes in natural environments, and improving project monitoring. But conservation groups claim that the agencies have again fallen short of their responsibilities; the guidelines are not mandatory, and the five-point plan creates only the illusion of reform.

Controversial HCPs have been granted to the Plum Creek Timber Company for widespread clear-cutting in the Cascade Range, allowing the company to take northern spotted owls, grizzly bears, and Canada lynx, among dozens of other species. In an HCP that Klippstein describes as the worst ever granted, International Paper has been allowed to disturb the habitat of the few remaining red-cockaded woodpeckers, trading a small portion of their habitat for the right to log off more than 5 million acres of this endangered species' habitat. Two toll roads passing through "protected" areas designated by NCCPs in southern California disturb crucial areas for endangered species such as the arroyo toad, the gnatcatcher, and the Stephens' kangaroo rat.

## Planning More Development

Not far from Crystal Cove, Monica Florian explains over the steady clamor of bulldozers that we are standing beside a nature reserve set aside by the Irvine Company, where she is senior vice president. The company has built the largest master-planned urban environment in the United States on massive landholdings that it acquired in its cattle-ranching days. It has created communities that together house 200,000 residents. More are in the planning stage, and the construction of others, such as this block of Newport Coast, is under way.

Here, in the Newport Hills Development, a swath of three-story homes rises like a king's court above the ocean views on one side of the reserve. Protected space, dotted with cell phone towers and criss-crossed with small roadways, lies on the other. That space is part of 38,000 acres set aside from development; the Irvine Company is free to build on the remainder of its 216,000-acre regional holdings. The set-aside includes 17,000 acres of public land combined with 21,000 acres of land from the Irvine Company—only 4,000 acres of which were not previously under some sort of protection. The reserve system, making up the Nature Reserve of Orange County, is designed to safeguard 40 rare species in what is now the largest remaining habitat block in the county.

Florian admits that the NCCP process and the federal no-surprises guarantees are what it took to bring companies such as hers willingly to the planning table. "To address endangered-species issues," she says, "we have to find a way to deal with them on private land. The NCCP seemed like a better way to do business."

Business indeed. But how much should private business concerns be allowed to extract from the environment, and how much should be left for the less defined public, or environmental, good? Even before the NCCPs went into place allowing development on coastal sage scrub inhabited by the gnatcatcher and other rare species, only 10 percent of the region's sage scrub habitat remained. "When we say there's only 10 percent of this area left," says Klippstein, "that means there's 10 pieces of the pie and 9 of them are gone. When developers come in and say, 'We want the last piece,' you stab them with a fork and say, 'No, you've already had 9.'"

# PROTECTING ENDANGERED SPECIES WHEN THEY CROSS THE U.S.-CANADIAN BORDER

Gary Turbak

In the following selection, freelance journalist Gary Turbak reports that endangered species do not enjoy the same legal protection they have in the United States once they cross the border into Canada. Species such as marbled murrelets, woodland caribou, and lynx can be found in the United States and Canada, he writes. However, while these species are considered endangered in America, Turbak relates, in Canada they may not be classified as needing protection. Grizzly bears, for example, are more abundant in Canada than the United States—meaning that if a grizzly crosses from the United States into Canada, it could become a legal target for hunters, the author explains. Despite these differences in the law, Turbak reports that the United States and Canada have worked together to preserve some species, such as gray wolves. Turbak remains hopeful that the two countries will continue to work together to protect endangered species on both sides of the border. Turbak contributes to magazines such as *National Wildlife* and the *American Legion*.

The grizzly moved steadily north, periodically resting and feeding in the Montana forest. Eventually, the bear reached the international boundary, for a moment standing with its head in Canada and its rear in the United States. It didn't know it, but its situation had just changed drastically. In Canada, the grizzly is legally hunted and its habitat is more readily compromised than in the Lower 48.

Unlike the United States, which safeguards species under the federal Endangered Species Act (ESA), Canada has no such national law. U.S. conservationists see this as problematic for wide-ranging northern species such as grizzlies, caribou, wolves, lynx and others, which range on both sides of the border. "Most people don't realize it, but many U.S. endangered species are at risk when they cross into Canada," says

Gary Turbak, "Walking the Line," *National Wildlife*, October/November 2002. Copyright © 2002 by National Wildlife Federation. Reproduced by permission.

John Kostyack, National Wildlife Federation (NWF) senior counsel.

Canada's imperiled species list—compiled by the Committee on the Status of Endangered Wildlife in Canada (COSEWIC), an independent, government-appointed group of scientists, academics, wildlife managers and conservationists—currently includes 53 mammals and 52 birds (plus 275 other plants and animals). But it carries no legal weight. And while all the provinces have wildlife laws on the books, "protection is sporadic and limited," says Sandy Baumgartner, a spokesperson at the Canadian Wildlife Federation, one of the country's largest environmental organizations. "Historically, the laws apply only to fish and game species. Others may be theoretically protected, but the legislative teeth to enforce the laws may not exist."

## Enacting Species Protection in Canada

To keep species from falling through the gaps, environmentalists on both sides of the border are calling for Canada to enact a national species protection law. It's been tried before—three times since 1995, in fact. Each time the bill was dropped by the Canadian Parliament due to elections, which automatically cancel pending legislation.

[In 2002] another form of the bill—the Species At Risk Act (SARA) —[was] before Parliament. [SARA became law in June 2003.] Some Canadian conservationists criticize the bill for not going far enough, while others are backing it, in part because they are concerned that the opportunity won't come up again. "After so many failed attempts we certainly don't want this bill to die," says Baumgartner. Some last minute attempts have strengthened the bill, but habitat protection is still an issue. "After all," she says, "what good does it do to protect a species that has no place to go?"

Take the marbled murrelet, for example, a U.S. threatened species that the Canadian Wildlife Service (CWS) calls "the most mysterious bird on the Pacific coast of Canada." This quail-sized seabird—which swims with its bill pointed skyward—migrates up and down the Pacific coast from northern California to British Columbia.

Most of the year, murrelets make their living diving for small fish, with stubby wings working like flippers. But after mating in spring, these birds make an astounding journey. Flying as far as 50 miles inland, they build nests 60 to 80 feet off the ground in ancient fir or spruce trees—no small feat for birds with webbed feet. The female lays a single egg, and for the next month the pair takes turns keeping it warm. Each night, the "off-duty" bird returns from the sea to start its shift at the nest, and its mate heads for the coast to feed. So secretive are these birds about their nests that only once (in 1990) have observers in British Columbia seen one of the province's 45,000 or so marbled murrelets on its nest.

While predators such as falcons and owls kill some murrelets, and others die after becoming entangled in fishing nets or blundering into oil spills, the murrelets' single greatest threat is the logging of old-growth forests where they nest. COSEWIC lists them as threatened; SARA surely would include them as an at-risk species. But without a law that provides for the protection of their habitat, their future is uncertain. [In] summer [2000], for example, the government of British Columbia sold the logging rights to a marbled murrelet nesting area north of Vancouver—even subsidizing the sale.

## Critically Endangered Caribou

Another group of imperiled, part-time residents of British Columbia are members of a small herd of woodland caribou that lives part of the year in the Selkirk Mountains of northern Idaho and northeastern Washington—the only caribou that range in the Lower 48. A subspecies closely related to its tundra-dwelling cousins, the caribou is a medium-sized member of the deer family. A large male might weigh as much as 600 pounds; a female is about half that size.

As their name suggests, woodland caribou live in mountain forests, where they dine on arboreal lichens, glass, forbs and huckleberry bushes. In early winter, the animals move to lower elevations to avoid deep snow. As the season progresses, however, they climb back up to ridges above 6,000 feet, where their oversized hooves trod the now-hardened, 6-to-12-foot-high snowpack to reach otherwise inaccessible lichens far up in the trees. Except for mountain goats, woodland caribou are the only large animals that tough out winter in the high country.

Prior to 1900, woodland caribou occupied parts of most northern-tier states, plus a huge swath of territory across wooded Canada. Their numbers have since declined throughout Canada, and one by one the U.S. populations have blinked out, leaving only the Selkirk herd. When surveys in the 1980s put this population at 25 or 30 animals, U.S. authorities listed the woodland caribou as endangered and began to augment the herd with transplants from Canada. Although 103 Canadian caribou have thus far been added, the herd still numbers only about 30 animals.

Because of the species' poor survival rate, authorities . . . pulled the plug on the relocation program. Now, the Selkirk caribou are considered the most critically endangered mammals in the United States. "We are slowly and surely getting in a precarious position," says Jon Almack, a biologist with Washington's Department of Fish and Wildlife.

The reasons are many. Relatively unwary, woodland caribou make easy targets for poachers or hunters who may mistake them for deer or elk. And cows don't breed until they are three years old and then usually produce only one calf a year. But the major problem is loss of habitat, primarily from timber harvesting. Logging has also opened up the forest for deer, boosting their numbers in many areas. More deer mean more predators.

Because the Selkirk herd is federally protected in the United States, its welfare is commonly considered in land decisions. In Canada, however, authorities have done little to protect caribou habitat near the border. In 2000, a natural gas pipeline was pushed through the herd's range just a few miles north of the boundary, where logging regularly takes place. "We're losing habitat right and left on the British Columbia side of the border," says Almack.

## Species on the Border

Other "transboundary" species at risk because of habitat loss are as varied as wolverines, bull trout, spotted owls, piping plovers and lynx, the reclusive cats that eke out a living by hunting snowshoe hares. In central and northern Canada, lynx populations are healthy. Along the Canadian-U.S. border and possibly into Wyoming, Utah and Colorado, only small populations exist—perhaps fewer than 700 cats total. As a result, they are listed as threatened under the ESA.

Lynx are primarily denizens of the northern woods, where hares abound and deep snow makes travel difficult for competing predators. Their oversized feet act like snowshoes, keeping them atop the drifts while other carnivores sink. But at the southern edge of their range, less snow reduces the cats' advantage, and the relatively mild-mannered felines must compete with more aggressive predators such as bobcats and coyotes. Consequently, the lynx's stronghold lies well north of the border, where its population fluctuates in synchrony with hare numbers, which ebb about every ten years. When forced to strike out in search of food, a lynx's journey can cover hundreds of miles and extend south of the border. "The lower 48 states' populations are highly dependent on lynx coming from Canada," says U.S. Fish and Wildlife Service (FWS) biologist Lori Nordstrom.

Because its population is stable in Canada, the lynx almost certainly will not be granted protection under SARA. "Right now, that lack of protection is not a problem," says Nordstrom.

"But if lynx numbers were ever severely reduced in Canada, populations of the cats in the Lower 48 would suffer." In the meantime, any of the cats that wander from the United States into Canada are fair game for trappers.

## The Fate of Grizzlies

Of all the transboundary creatures, the grizzly is the species that most concerns U.S. conservationists. "Grizzlies cross the U.S.-Canadian border a lot and as far as we know, no one ever checks their papers," says FWS wildlife biologist Wayne Kasworm. At least half of the 25 grizzlies radio-collared by biologists in one part of northern Montana have spent time in Canada—including one itinerant bruin that reputedly ventured 20 to 25 miles on each side of the border, denning every year in the nation he happened to occupy when winter hit.

Fewer than 1,000 of the huge bears (down from an estimated high of 100,000) are thought to exist in the lower 48 states, with four of five remaining populations straddling the Canadian border. Two of these populations, in Montana and Idaho, have so few bears that one biologist has called them "the walking dead."

Although grizzlies can be fierce predators, the bulk of their diet consists of roots, berries, insects and carrion. An adult grizzly can put away 30 pounds of food a day in the summer, and during the autumn pre-hibernation feeding frenzy that amount may triple. "This prodigious food requirement, along with the fact that these bears generally avoid one another lest a fight occur, requires them to maintain large home ranges that often span hundreds of square miles—and the border," says Sterling Miller, a bear expert and NWF biologist.

In the United States, federal law protects grizzlies. But when they enter Canada, where grizzlies are not considered at risk, they can he hunted in most jurisdictions—or pursued illegally. In 1996, for example, Montana grizzly number 355 dropped off the radar screen soon after receiving a radio collar. Flying over southern Canada the following spring, Kasworm picked up the bear's signal and followed it to where the collar lay hidden in the brush. The device had been cut off with a knife, and the ground lay splattered with blood. The exact fate of grizzly 355 is unknown—what is known is that no one removes a collar from a live grizzly.

Authorities in British Columbia seem particularly uncertain about how to handle the grizzly hunting question. In February 2001, officials in the province issued what was to be a three-year moratorium on killing the bears. But with the ink barely dry on that edict, a newly elected provincial government lifted the ban that July.

Even so, hunting is certainly not the biggest threat to grizzlies. "Habitat degradation is even more insidious," says Kasworm. On both sides of the border, roads—often built in connection with logging, mining or energy exploration—fragment habitat. One southern Alberta study found more than four miles of road per square mile of habitat, a ratio thought to be several times higher than what grizzlies can tolerate.

## Traveling Wolves

More adaptable are gray wolves that, like grizzlies, routinely traverse the border. Abundant in Canada, wolves are considered endangered or threatened south of the border. Persecution from governments and livestock interests had virtually eliminated wolves from the Lower 48 (with the exception of the Great Lakes region) by the 1930s. But after gaining protection under the ESA, a few wanderers began crossing from Canada into Montana in 1979. One such group—dubbed the Magic Pack—denned in Glacier National Park in 1986, producing the first wolf pups born in the western United States in about 50 years.

"Now it's not uncommon for a Canadian wolf to cross the border, find a bride, then return to Canada and vice versa," says Ed Bangs, wolf recovery coordinator for FWS. One wolf traveled several hundred miles from Banff National Park in Alberta to Idaho, hung around a few months, then went back.

Most border-dwelling packs den in Canada and enter the United States to hunt, traveling as far as 20 miles a day—within a home range that can span 300 miles—searching for moose, deer or other animals large enough to feed everyone. Five packs have home ranges that straddle the border, which means the same wolves protected under the ESA south of the border are considered fur bearers, game animals or worse in Canada. "Wolves that cross the border from Montana and Idaho can be shot as vermin," says Stephen Legault, executive director of Wildcanada.net, a grassroots environmental organization.

Several dozen American-reared wolves have been killed after crossing the border, and FWS researchers confirm that legal kills in Canada are a leading cause of death for wolves radio-collared in the United States. Between 1987 and 1998, Canadians took a dozen collared American wolves, three times the number that died of natural causes.

## Working Together to Save Species

Still, Canada and the United States do have a long history of cooperating to help wolves. The wolves released in Yellowstone National Park and Idaho in the mid-1990s came from Canada and were key to the U.S. recovery program. Also important is the ongoing genetic link between the two wolf groups. "We've tried to make the U.S. Northern Rockies population an extension of the Canadian mass of wolves to keep Montana, Idaho and Wyoming wolves healthy and free of genetic inbreeding," says Bangs.

Canada has also taken significant steps on its own to protect and recover the peregrine falcon, trumpeter swan and other imperiled species. Perhaps most notable is the country's resurrection of the prairie-dwelling swift fox. As the smallest wild canine in North America—weighing about half as much as a house cat—the swift fox historically claimed the short-grass prairie from southern Canada to Texas, preying on mice, voles, birds, ground squirrels and prairie dogs. But decades of habitat loss, coyote predation, trapping and poisoning (mostly as accidental victims of anti-wolf and coyote campaigns) greatly reduced populations of the animals on both sides of the border. The swift fox disappeared entirely from Canada in the 1930s, and in the United States, this diminutive carnivore became a candidate for the threatened species list in 1995.

To save the species, Canadian authorities began an aggressive captive-breeding program in 1983 and eventually more than 900 swift foxes were released into their traditional southern Alberta and Saskatchewan hunting grounds. Before long, people reported seeing swift foxes across the border in Montana, an area where the animals had disappeared decades ago. "To everyone's surprise, Canadian foxes were traveling up to 30 miles, effectively changing their 'citizenship,'" says Brian Giddings, furbearer coordinator for Montana Fish, Wildlife and Parks.

The thriving Montana population today contains about 225 foxes, and [in 2001] U.S. authorities decided the swift fox was no longer a threatened species candidate. Canada's restoration also achieved great success, with about 700 swift foxes living where once there were none. Still, survival of the swift fox is not guaranteed. Without a national law to protect its habitat, the fox's continued existence depends on provincial governments and the largesse of private landowners—all of which may have other priorities.

For the swift fox, the grizzly and other at-risk wildlife species that hold a sort of "dual citizenship," a lot depends upon what Canada does now to ensure their future. The United States enacted its federal legislation nearly 30 years ago. While far from perfect, the law prevented the extinction of many of the species listed under its protection.

Some, such as the bald eagle and peregrine falcon, have even recovered. A national law in Canada could produce similar successes, while also providing safe passage for those creatures that cross over to the neighbor's turf. After all, Canada may share a border with the United States, but in the end, the countries are connected even more by their rich wildlife legacies.

CHAPTER 4

# THE FIGHT TO SAVE
# ENDANGERED SPECIES

# RACING TO SAVE THE SONORAN PRONGHORN

Ben Ikenson

Ben Ikenson is the editor in chief of *Fish and Wildlife News*, the
U.S. Fish and Wildlife Service's quarterly newsletter. He has also
written for publications such as *Earth Island Journal* and *Americas*.
In this selection, Ikenson relates the struggles faced by the endangered Sonoran pronghorn, a goatlike hoofed animal. While pronghorn were once numerous throughout the western United States
and Mexico, Ikenson reports, now only a handful remain in the
wild. The author explains that habitat fragmentation caused by
roads, overgrazing, and drought are some of the biggest obstacles
the species faces. However, Ikenson continues, efforts are being
made by government organizations on the U.S. and Mexican sides
of the border to ensure the pronghorn's survival—and conservation biologists are hopeful about the pronghorn's future.

At the U.S.-Mexico border in southwestern Arizona, the old Peli-
groso/Danger signs dangling from the barbed wire do little to stop a
furtive flood of foot traffic through the desert, despite its unforgiving
conditions. In fact, this was the grim scene where fourteen undocu-
mented Mexican immigrants tragically perished in May 2001, and
where more than two hundred have since perished in the searing heat.

But while people are ill-equipped to survive the harsh conditions of
the Sonoran Desert, a subspecies that has inhabited the region since
well before human history, the Sonoran pronghorn, may be even less
able to handle the modern, widespread consequences of human activity there. In conjunction with . . . extended periods of low rainfall
during hot summer months, range fragmentation and habitat degradation are presenting serious problems for the Sonoran pronghorn,
which was listed as an endangered species in 1967.

A goatlike animal often mistaken for a relative of the African antelope, the Sonoran pronghorn is one of five subspecies within the
unique Antilocapridae family. The species descended from prehistoric
antilocaprids, who roamed North America during the Eocene epoch

some thirty million years ago. By the end of the Pleistocene, all were extinct but one: the pronghorn (*Antilocapra americana*).

## The Fastest Mammal

The fastest land mammal in North America, and possibly the second fastest in the world after the African cheetah, pronghorn can reach speeds of up to sixty miles per hour. Unlike the cheetah, who tires after a quarter-mile burst of energy, the pronghorn can maintain its top speed for about four minutes, and clip along steadily at thirty miles per hour for up to five miles.

Scientists believe the Sonoran pronghorn developed its extraordinary speed and stamina millions of years ago, when the continent was populated with swift, large carnivores, including saber-toothed cats, lions, and two species of American cheetah. These have since gone extinct, leaving healthy adult pronghorn free from all but the craftiest predators.

In more recent times, pronghorn became a regular component of the human diet for nomadic Native Americans such as the Shoshoni, the Bannock, the Ute, the Paiute, and the Gostiute. These tribes came together annually for three weeks to partake in a great pronghorn drive, forming a large circle and closing it inward until the prey could be harvested. Beyond mere sustenance though, the hunt functioned as a cultural celebration whereby cross-tribal marriages were arranged and spiritual rites were conducted.

A Blackfeet legend tells how the pronghorn came to inhabit the prairie: When the Creator turned the animal loose on the slopes of the Rockies, its great speed was not suited to the tricky terrain, where it stumbled and fell. The pragmatic Creator hastily relocated the pronghorn to the prairie where it flourished, at least for a while.

## Slaughtering the Pronghorn

But by the turn of the twentieth century, the entire pronghorn species, which had numbered as high as forty million, was reduced to twenty thousand. Evidently, nothing in nature could prepare the pronghorn for the introduction of a relatively modern human invention: the rifle. Hunting in the nineteenth and twentieth centuries greatly contributed to the rapid decline of the entire species. Market hunters slaughtered millions of pronghorn and continued to do so even after the value of the meat diminished because it was so plentiful. Often, carcasses were simply left to rot wherever bullets brought them down.

As settlers cleared land and staked fences, pronghorn, which unlike deer, will not jump fences, were finding less forage and less room to roam. Also, many ranchers shot pronghorn, believing, falsely, that they competed with livestock for forage. Pronghorn typically don't eat the grasses favored by livestock. But the gradual overgrazing of grasses by livestock inhibited growth of the symbiotic pronghorn forage and led to illnesses such as blue tongue and epizootic hemorrhagic disease in cattle, and to ever-increasing habitat fragmentation.

Although all five subspecies suffered dramatically under the myriad pressures, the Sonoran pronghorn were reduced to perhaps the smallest number. Today, there are fewer than five hundred animals.

As much an icon of the Sonoran Desert as the buffalo, the Sonoran pronghorn likely once graced the landscape in small bands of twenty-five or so, roaming like caravans across vast expanses of the North American desert, throughout what is now southwestern Arizona, southeastern California, northeastern Baja California Norte, and northwestern Sonora, Mexico. About the size of small deer, bucks weigh between 100 and 130 pounds; does weigh between 75 to 100 pounds. With long legs, they are mostly beige in color with distinctive white stripes on their necks. Males show black cheek patches across their bony faces and boast the signature pronged horns, considerably larger than the females'.

## Rare in the Wild

Of course, seeing Sonoran pronghorn in the wild has become increasingly rare. Of the small number remaining, there are three isolated populations: two in Mexico and one confined to federal lands in the United States, including Cabeza Prieta National Wildlife Refuge in Arizona, where U.S. Fish and Wildlife Service biologist John Morgart tracks and monitors the herd.

"It's life versus death out here," Morgart says. A glimpse through his high-powered binoculars confirms the ominous statement. The only perceivable movement in the wide desert valley is that of two rival buzzards poking for morsels at the underside of a sunbleached skeleton. The sound of competing wings slices the silence like erratic drumbeats.

Those who claim this vast Sonoran Desert arena as home—the turkey vulture, the desert bighorn sheep, the coyote, the desert tortoise, the saguaro cactus, and the Sonoran pronghorn—have evolved over time to survive under notoriously austere conditions. To travel long distances in response to rainfall across a landscape teeming with hungry predators, the pronghorn adapted two distinctive survival techniques: great speed and a pair of enormous eyes positioned for a wide-ranging view. Its vision is said to rival a pair of strong binoculars. However, these evolutionary attributes may not be enough; the dwindling pronghorn who gaze with curiously large eyes upon the landscape are blind to an onslaught of threats that may be impossible to outrun.

All three populations of Sonoran pronghorn contend with roads, fencing, and railroad tracks. Although the U.S. population and Mexico's northernmost population on the El Pinacate Biosphere Reserve can roam within a mile's distance of each other, border fencing and Mexico's Highway 2, which parallels the border, have divided them as effectively as if they inhabited separate continents. Further south, the largest population of some three hundred individuals—more than 60 percent of the entire population—is isolated by the Gulf of California on one side and Mexico's Highway 8 on the other.

## Altering Pronghorn Habitat

Border-dwelling pronghorn are challenged by the ongoing legacy of human and drug trafficking. Human foot traffic often means not only the disruption of pronghorn stomping grounds but also hazardous disturbances, including abandoned vehicles whose corrosive batteries and leaking fluids are known to contaminate the soil.

Still more menacing than the foot traffic, though, are the makeshift roads that litter both sides of the border. John Hervert, a wildlife program manager for the Arizona Game and Fish Department, has observed some of the more subtle and long-lasting deterioration caused by the network of illegal roads. "On more heavily used roads, the hydrology is being altered to the detriment of plants," he says. "On first glance, you can see how a road crushes plants or cuts through the natural flow of vegetation. But even worse is what you cannot see right away. The movement of water in slightly sloping desert valleys is very slow, and heavily used roads will effectively divert moisture away from lower level vegetation." In short, pronghorn forage dies where roads make incisions across the land.

Additionally, overgrazing has taken a toll on native vegetation, particularly in the El Pinacate Biosphere Reserve, where hungry livestock wander over from a neighboring ejido (communal agricultural unit) and deplete the greenery, leaving the soil especially vulnerable to erosion. Much of the native vegetation that pronghorn graze, such as dune bursage, mistletoe, and mesquite leaves, is vanishing at an accelerated pace, giving way to parched earth and shrub.

"We suspect that livestock grazing can significantly alter the equilibrium of the plant community, evidence of which exists on both sides of the border," says Hervert. "The dominance of creosote in certain areas is a good example of how the relative balance in the native plant ecology has been upset."

To Hervert, an overabundance of creosote is a reliable indicator that a desert ecosystem is in disrepair. A hearty, native desert shrub that provides forage for neither cattle nor pronghorn, creosote outcompetes neighboring palatable vegetation. By degrees, patches of the shrub will fan out, grow taller, and dominate an area. Ultimately, a landscape of thick, inedible vegetation is unattractive to an animal like the pronghorn, which prefers open vistas where it can use its extraordinary vision to spot predators while it forages.

In fact, wherever native habitat has been altered in its current, fragmented range, the Sonoran pronghorn suffers. And each factor that militates against the subspecies is made worse by the recent spate of dry seasons. Morgart says that with the extreme hot and dry conditions of the past several years, "border fencing and other obstacles are severe deterrents for an animal in search of nutritious forage and water." Worse still, adds Morgart, the harsh natural pattern of drought-like conditions in the Sonoran Desert is "possibly exacerbated by global warming." In other words, water will likely continue to be even more scarce than it has been historically in this region.

## Not Enough Rain

Even hearty desert animals need a minimum of moisture for survival, which adult pronghorn typically retrieve through their preferred forage. These plants spring up after rainfall, which the animals would instinctively follow were it not for the barrage of obstacles throughout their range. But hemmed in by barriers and struggling through six consecutive dry years in an already arid place, pronghorn are challenged to procure meaningful nutrition—and hydration—through second-choice forage that is scarce in moisture.

The drought is also significantly diminishing the animal's success at nurturing young. The better forage a mother can access, the more nutrients she can divert to her fetus. And after birth, the mother is better equipped to provide nutritious milk during the critical nursing stage. If malnourished, a fawn is likely to die. Because the pronghorn's life span is generally short, between ten and twelve years, the time it has to reproduce is precious.

Is hope for the pronghorn as diminished as the recent rainfall? "No," replies Morgart. "As long as we don't let our guard down."

Morgart heads a collaborative recovery team that includes scientists from both sides of the border. In the United States, the Fish and Wildlife Service, the Arizona Game and Fish Department, Organ Pipe Cactus National Monument, the U.S. Bureau of Land Management, the U.S. Air Force, the U.S. Marine Corps, and the University of Arizona are working for the pronghorn. Recovery team members from Mexico include El Pinacate Biosphere Reserve (PINA) and the Institute of Environment and Sustainable Development of the State of Sonora, Mexico (IMADES). Together the team's ultimate goals are to increase Sonoran pronghorn numbers and to improve and expand their current range.

"It's all been a cooperative effort," Morgart says. "We're collaring animals to track them. We're sharing our research and discussing ideas."

## International Cooperation

One of the more important achievements in Mexico has been the declaration of the PINA biosphere reserve as a national protected treasure . . . on June 10, 1993. "This reserve and other strategies orchestrated by the federal government to protect areas for the management and conservation of wildlife are good tools for Sonoran pronghorn recovery," says biologist Carlos Castillo, who directs activities for PINA. He also serves on the National Commission of Natural Protected Areas and coordinated Sonoran pronghorn recovery efforts in Mexico for ten years, from 1987 to 1997.

As managers of natural protected areas, PINA and IMADES staff are trying to learn more about the use of habitat and behavior ecology of the Sonoran pronghorn. Specifically, they are looking at the possible existence of biological corridors along Highways 2 and 8. Both highways may be widened to the detriment of conservation efforts. "We are trying to propose more restrictive regulations for the highway-widening process," says Castillo, "and also to develop some broad education programs for local communities to help them gain an appreciation for the importance of conservation."

The key to successful conservation of the Sonoran pronghorn, Castillo explains, is "binational cooperation, the search for common goals, and our collaborative skills to transmit the importance of the conservation of this species to the various stakeholders."

Of course, the challenges are still daunting to Castillo and his partners in Mexico. "The possibility that both Highway 2, between Sonoyta and San Luis Rio Colorado, and Highway 8, between Sonoyta and Puerto Penasco, may be widened pose as further barriers—in addition to border fencing—reducing potential for free movement and genetic exchange between Sonoran pronghorn in southwest Arizona and northwest Sonora," he says. "The drought that's been ongoing for years isn't helping either."

Back in the United States, biologists are working to alleviate the problems associated with the extreme dry conditions. Experimental techniques have been part of the process. For example, John Hervert and his colleagues from the Arizona Game and Fish Department have been hauling water tubs to remote areas on the wildlife refuge where they have tracked pronghorn activity. The four-mile-hikes with five-gallon jugs of water in 105-degree temperatures are proof of their dedication; the fact that the animals have responded is proof of their desperation, since they typically don't drink water when the moisture in their preferred forage is adequate.

The biologists have affixed cameras to snap pictures of activity at water tubs in an attempt to gather information on how to make them more effective. They are currently investigating the survival rate of fawns that have access to the water tubs as compared to those that do not.

Also, the adjacent Barry M. Goldwater Range, a military training ground used by the U.S. Air Force, plans to fund a forage-enhancement project on its land. Already the military, with support from the U.S. Bureau of Reclamation, drilled two test wells as a source of water for

the forage-enhancement project. One well was dry; the other fortunately hit water. Ground site preparation for the project was scheduled
to begin [in] August [2000]. By clearing creosote and watering areas
during below-average rainfall, biologists hope to increase the quantity
and quality of forage. If these efforts achieve the desired results, other
partners, including those in Mexico, may initiate similar projects
throughout pronghorn range.

## More Plans for Recovery

The recovery team has proposed several new activities in a recent
amendment to their recovery plan, believing that comprehensive doc-
umentation will provide the guidance necessary to increase pronghorn
survival and improve habitat. "It may be a long, hard road to recovery
ahead," says Morgart, "but the shorter road leads only to extinction."

To stave off extinction, the team is discussing the possibility of establishing a captive-breeding program. "We hope it doesn't come to
that," says Morgart. "We hope that conditions will improve enough
for pronghorn to reestablish their numbers on their own."

Only time—and the weather—can determine if conditions will improve. The winter months of 2000 and 2001 fortunately provided
more precipitation than in preceding years, and . . . surveys conducted by Arizona Game and Fish reveal that, as a consequence,
about fifty fawns were born into the U.S. population. The estimated
ratio of fawns to does revealed the highest productivity ever recorded
for Sonoran pronghorn. Up from an estimated total U.S. population
of 99 individuals in 2000, the U.S. pronghorn numbered approximately 140 in spring 2002, according to biologists, who factored some
adult mortality into their estimate. The most recent numbers for the
two populations in Mexico come from December 2000, where the total population estimate was 346.

Despite . . . spring [2002's] increase, Morgart remains circumspect.
"We still can't afford to assume that things are good," he says. "This
past winter has been extremely dry. In March, does began dropping
[giving birth to] fawns. There was not an adequate amount of rainfall
to allow for some green-up, nor was there an early and widespread
monsoon. Most of this season's fawns have probably died."

The Sonoran Desert presents an archetypal drama. It is, as Morgart
says, life versus death there. But modern circumstances threaten to
destroy some of the players completely. Over a relatively short period,
human actions have disturbed the evolutionary symbiosis honed over
eons to afford the natural inhabitants of this harsh land a fighting
chance. Pronghorn recovery efforts are a small step toward restoring
balance to this primordial stage.

# SAVING SPECTACLED BEARS IN PERU

Tui De Roy

In the following selection, author Tui De Roy details one Peruvian community's efforts to protect the spectacled bear. Lead by Heinz Plenge, a Peruvian wildlife photographer, and Bernie Peyton, a bear biologist from America, the community of Santa Catalina de Chongoyape near Mount Chaparri has dedicated itself to safeguarding habitat for the endangered bear, De Roy reports. Moreover, she writes, the village founded the Chaparri Private Ecological Reserve by donating 86 percent of its communal land for the project. She relates that Plenge and Peyton's leadership and the community's support have resulted in changed local attitudes about the bears. Instead of viewing the animals as a threat, as they had in the past, the villagers now work to rescue captive bears and, if possible, return them to the wild. New Zealand–based De Roy is a frequent contributor to magazines such as *National Wildlife* and *Geographical*.

We are in northern Peru searching for secretive spectacled bears. No luck so far. Instead, we awake to the mournful courtship calls of small, gray doves drifting up from a fog-filled valley and, closer by, the nervous buzz of a tiny amazilia hummingbird. But as I climb out of my sleeping bag, I survey our surroundings and discover that, in the failing light of dusk, we had inadvertently set up camp near clear signs of our quest: Etched in the smooth trunk of a sturdy tree are large, slashing claw marks. Not too long ago, a bear had climbed up to survey its territory.

For three days now, along with a small group of fellow bear enthusiasts, I have been skirting around a 4,500-foot-high, craggy rock formation called Mount Chaparri in hopes of just such a discovery. The claw marks are a palpable sign not only that bears are close by, but that a remarkable social experiment involving wildlife and people is working.

Mount Chaparri—which stretches from the foothills of the lofty Andean Cordillera into lowland desert plains like the sharp claw of a mountain-size dinosaur—is a key part of this endangered bear's range. The coastal desert gives way to a unique habitat of deciduous dry forest before rising into mountainous cloud forest further inland. No rain falls for at least nine months of the year, but cool mist wafts in over the lowlands from the distant sea. It is in these cloud forests along the steep Andes from Venezuela to Brazil that the bear typically lives.

For the people near Mount Chaparri, its imposing bulk has always commanded magical status. Until recently, only shamans dared live in its shadow, collecting herbs from its sacred flanks where bears and other wildlife found respite from heavy hunting pressures. But [in] December [2001], the mountain, along with 117 square miles of surrounding habitat, became the first legally declared private conservation reserve in Peru. In the process, the bear, which was once persecuted as a cattle predator, has morphed from villain to mascot in the locals' hearts.

## Saving the Bears

This history-making accomplishment is the work of two visionary men. One is Heinz Plenge, Peru's foremost wildlife photographer. The other is Bernie Peyton, a spectacled bear biologist from Berkeley, California—respected as the world expert on the species. Through their joint dreams, an unconventional scheme is emerging that will compensate local people for the wise stewardship of their wild heritage.

We get a firsthand sense of what's at stake as we continue our exploration. Our path takes us along a clear, gurgling stream up to its source in a steep-sided canyon, where desert frogs sing and wild tomatoes grow. While a majestic Andean condor sweeps low over our heads, we scramble up a precipitous arroyo to a knife-edge ridge between two watersheds.

Bear signs increase noticeably as we pass close under the brooding presence of Mount Chaparri and descend into the valley on the other side: Here, a young pasallo tree shredded for the tender, edible pulp inside its trunk; there, a patch of ripe nightshade berries where a bear fed and left droppings. Still, we spot no wild bears, although it is likely that they have been watching us.

To see the animals, we must complete the loop back to our starting point, a spacious, quasi-natural rehabilitation center, tucked away in a secluded valley. The place serves as a halfway home for bears rescued from illegal captivity. Nearby, a discreet house constructed of straw-colored adobe overlooks a permanent spring-fed stream.

Here I find Heinz Plenge. A soft-spoken Peeavian whose great-grandparents came from Germany, Plenge is putting the finishing touches on his new solar-powered home in the wilderness. Over lunch he tells me his story. "It all started three years ago," he begins. "I'd just turned 50 and knew I couldn't spend the rest of my days trudging though mountains and jungles to take pictures." His dream was to find a quiet place surrounded by wildlife where he'd be able to point his camera out the window even in his old age.

Having traveled and worked in every last corner of Peru, Plenge returned to his roots in the northern dry forest where he'd cut his teeth as a wildlife photographer. When, to his delight, he discovered that bears still clung to the hinterlands, he approached the local farming community of Santa Catalina de Chongoyape—where 2,000 or so dirt-poor and downtrodden residents held communal title to their marginal lands.

## A Community Plan

Plenge had devised an ingenious, simple plan. After weeks of patiently attending community meetings, he slowly laid out his ideas to win over skeptical locals: He would help them organize to defend their rights if in return they would adopt long-term goals to safeguard their resources and environment. They listened and Plenge delivered, wresting water rights from politicians and officials who had favored ambitious agricultural schemes over the needs of poor farmers. For the first time, community residents could start irrigating their fields from a reservoir in their valley. To safeguard the watershed, the community, in turn, would cease cutting the trees from surrounding hillsides.

Plenge also offered to organize cattle-owning community members so they could legally expel thousands of cows belonging to outsiders who paid no fees while over-grazing the arid commons. He also argued that if the local people would get together to suspend hunting in the region for a few years, and likewise prevent outsiders from doing so, they'd be able to set aside a small hunting preserve when deer numbers rose. Then they could sell guiding services and hefty deer-shooting licenses to city slickers.

Plenge's notions captured the community's imagination, and the scheme took off. Soon residents allowed him to build his dream retreat at the foot of the mountain. Within a few more months of deliberations, the delegates voted to set aside their non-arable lands—86 percent of their community property—as the legally bound Chaparri Private Ecological Reserve.

## Rescuing Captive Bears

It was at this time that a couple of timely coincidences conspired to bring the bears back into the picture. Out of the blue, Plenge got a call from his long-time friend, bear-specialist Peyton, whom he hadn't seen in years. "Heinz, I've been a researcher all my life," Peyton told Plenge. "Now I want to do something more creative." At the same time, news reached Plenge that a captive bear was about to be confiscated by the government agency in charge of wildlife and natural resources.

"Everything happened very fast after that," recalls Plenge. Peyton came down from California and the bear, a young female named "Linda" (or "Yinda" depending on local pronunciation), was taken to Chaparri, where the community welcomed her as a symbol of their new direction. The two men dug deep into their own pockets to build a natural enclosure guarded by solar-powered electric fencing where the animal could roam freely and find wild foods to supplement a balanced diet prepared daily by a full-time caretaker.

Not long after, a country circus rumbled into Chongoyape town, where it was met not by cheers of delight but by an angry crowd that summoned the police to confiscate an illegal show bear. Suddenly the Chaparri project became a local media sensation, and more rescued bears were proffered. Subsequently, when a mining company—BHP Billinton—learned about the residents' ecological resolve, it gave the community back 65,000 acres of prime agricultural land it had acquired earlier.

By the time we finish talking, the sun is sinking over Chaparri's shoulder, and shadows rustling in the thickets announce the presence of a growing number of wild desert foxes in another of Plenge's innovative schemes. He has discovered that they love nothing better than the seed pods of the native acacia trees extirpated in past years from much of the landscape. The pods are sold by the sackful as horse fodder, and Plenge buys them and strews them across the plain from the back of his old Isuzu 4x4, letting the foxes, which excrete the seeds, do the reforestation work that would otherwise cost a fortune.

Never short of ideas, he keeps conceiving of more and more schemes to restore the local ecosystem to its former health. From a zoo in the capital of Lima he has . . . brought 26 deer to bolster the wild population. Peccaries should be next, and a herd of locally extinct guanacos has been promised from another region where there are still wild herds. Andean condors will receive a helping hand with deliveries of supplemental food—marine mammal carcasses that have naturally washed up on beaches. The turkeylike white-winged guans, which had disappeared for a century until a few were rediscovered 30 years ago, will be reintroduced into the wild.

## Keeping the Momentum Going

If Plenge is the conductor who is driving this train of change, Peyton is its engineer, bringing technical know-how from the outside world to lube the machinery and make sure it doesn't stall.

The two men were together 25 years ago when Peyton, as a young student, spotted his first wild bear in Chaparri. Now Peyton is dedicating his every resource into furthering the Chaparri project as a model of sustainable use. "To me, conservation means hiring locals, improving their education, taking care of their real needs and providing the dignity they deserve," he says.

Not everything about their plan has been easy. In some outlying sections of the community, persecution of wild bears continued unabated. So Plenge came up with the idea of harnessing the local fervor for football (soccer). With the help of local leaders, he organized a big

tournament and named it the "Bear's Cup." Only villages that
pledged to protect bears could participate. Peyton designed an engag-
ing logo of a bear clutching a football for team jersey—17 men's, 17
women's and 14 children's teams to date—and carved bronze bear tro-
phies to award winners. It was a roaring success.

But much work remains to he done. Education and health care still
must be brought to the local people, a management plan is needed
and new financial opportunities must be sought for the community.
Peyton is especially concerned with involving the women and children as he is passionate about rewarding their dedication with tangi-
ble benefits. "These people have been ignored for centuries," Peyton
says. "They are like a seed in the desert waiting for just a little nour-
ishment to flourish."

A fund-raising program is desperately needed as both men have ex-
hausted their personal resources to maintain momentum. Grant proposals are flying and some donations are arriving. An adopt-a-bear
program is about to be launched, and long-term research proposals
are being drawn up. Already Peyton and Plenge are thinking about
bears and people in other regions and are scoping out possibilities for
two other similar projects in other parts of Peru.

## Returning to the Wild

Early one morning I find a beautiful male bear in his prime laid out
luxuriously on a sun-warmed rock, just as the cool morning fog dissi-
pates around him. His name is "Cuto," and he looks wild and free—
almost. He yawns lazily, his long, pink tongue stretching in a big curl,
then blinks slowly as he surveys the tranquil valley below. His black
fur gleams with health. When he turns his head, he reveals the
unique white pattern around his muzzle and eyes, which differs in
each individual and gives the species its name.

If all goes well, one day soon either Cuto or some of the other bears
housed here may be searching the semi-desert scrub for native berries,
or climbing the fawn-colored ramparts of Mount Chaparri in search
of their very favorite food—the tender hearts of giant aerial bromeliad
plants growing on the sheer rock faces. But there are serious scientific
and management questions which must still be answered—like finding out which gene pool Cuto belongs to, whether he'll be able to
fend for himself in the wild and, crucially, if his tameness will not
turn him into a "problem bear," raiding farmers' crops and livestock
rather than heading for the hills.

Linda, the first captive to come to the facility, has already made her
transition to the wild successfully. Only a few months after she arrived, she escaped. A month later she was recaptured, then escaped
again. The next time she was sighted, she was ushering a small cub
ahead of her up the valley, proving beyond doubt that making the
readjustment to a wild existence after long confinement is quite feasi-

ble. Whenever she is spotted in the plains, rather than fetch their shotguns as they might have once done, cattlemen watch over her until she returns to the safety of the canyons.

Other residents at the bear facility may face less ambitious futures, their age and terrible scars from years of cruel captivity make them poor candidates for life in the wild. One of these is "Domingo," a white-muzzled, 30-year-old veteran who spent the bulk of his life in a small cage. He had been given barely enough food to stay alive. Although this has left him arthritic and partially blind, he still commands dominant status among the other bears. And his thick, shiny fur reflects his new healthy diet of fruit, gruel and corn—which he gets in addition to a total of 38 wild bear foods available in the five-acre natural enclosures.

Domingo now spends his days in blissful repose in a cool, man-made cave—retirement in paradise—emerging only for his morning stroll or to receive a few corn cobs from his protector. After a life of misery, he is at peace now. Plenge smiles as the bear takes the offerings gently from his fingers. No words are needed to describe a dream come true.

# PRESERVING OCELOTS IN SOUTH TEXAS

Adele Conover

In this selection, science journalist Adele Conover describes how endangered ocelots (leopardlike members of the cat family) are managing to survive in dwindling habitats in southern Texas. The cats used to be numerous in Texas, as well as Louisiana, Arkansas, and Arizona, Conover explains, but hunting and habitat destruction have combined to severely reduce the ocelot population. However, Conover reports that scientists, ranchers, and the government are working together to preserve and protect ocelot habitat. One of the gravest challenges facing ocelots is finding a territory, the author relates, and many ocelots have been killed crossing the many roads that run through their habitat or contending with other elements of human encroachment. Nevertheless, researchers are reporting that ocelots are establishing new territories, giving them hope for the cat's future. Adele Conover is a frequent contributor to *Smithsonian*. Her work has also appeared in *National Geographic for Kids*, *Ranger Rick*, and *National Wildlife*.

Peering through the thick, thorny south Texas brush, I can barely make out a feline form, its superb, spotted coat making it all but invisible. For nearly an hour, the creature stares at me in my pickup truck, ignoring a steady stream of vehicles crammed with bird-watchers bumping past on the road.

Suddenly, the cat—about twice the size of an ordinary tabby—rises, elegantly arches its back and glares at me one last time. Then, with the haughty grace of a fashion model, this rare Texas ocelot melts into the brush.

It was two decades ago that pioneer researcher Michael Tewes, now 44, came here to the Granjeno Research Natural Area, on the edge of the Laguna Atascosa National Wildlife Refuge (LANWR), as a graduate student on a lonely quest to find and study the Texas ocelot. Some biologists thought that it had been wiped out in the United States long before. "My ecology professor bet me a fifth of Jack Daniels I'd never find 'em,'" says Tewes, now coordinator of the Feline Research Program at the Caesar Kleburg Wildlife Research Institute at Texas A&M University-Kingsville.

The professor lost, of course, partly because of the disappearing act I saw in Granjeno, which is characteristic of the ocelot. By retreating into congenial environments, it has managed to survive not only in Texas but also in the remaining forests and thickets of Mexico and Central and South America. No one knows how many ocelots there are in the world, but Tewes says the population in Texas is somewhere between 80 and 120. Perhaps 30 to 40 reside in and around LANWR, while the rest are concentrated 40 miles to the north on several ranches that provide friendly refuge.

## Hunting and Habitat Loss

At one time the dappled cat's range in the United States extended across much of Texas, as well as Louisiana, Arkansas and Arizona. Everywhere, however, its tawny hide—a "most wonderful tangle of [blackish] stripes, bars, chains, spots, dots, and smudges," as naturalist and writer Ernest Thompson Seton once described it—was an irresistible prize. Seton added that a "trapper, frontiersman, or saddle-dandy of the sunny Rio Grande Plains did not consider himself dressed unless the silver of his gear was shining on a background of soft gray fur, the black-blotched velvet robe of an Ocelot." Bird painter John J. Audubon's son, J.W., who called ocelots "Leopard-Cats," noted that their "beautiful skin makes a most favorite bullet pouch." At one point, more than 200,000 ocelots were killed each year for their skins.

In 1980, an ocelot coat, requiring the hides of as many as 12 animals, sold for as much as $40,000. Although the cats are protected now in most places by the Convention on International Trade in Endangered Species (CITES), poaching still takes a toll.

But it is the steady loss of ocelot habitat that devastated their population in Texas. The same soil that supports ocelot-friendly thickets also makes wonderful farmland. "Obviously, humans and wildlife were competing for the same areas," says Tewes.

Once, "clearing that land must have been horribly hard," says Texas rancher Michael Corbett, 52, whose grandfather tamed his corner of the thorny landscape with axes and hired hands back in 1918. But bulldozers and other machines have made the brush easier to control. "As a result, since the 1920s more than 95 percent of the native thorn-scrub communities in the lower Rio Grande Valley have been converted for agricultural or urban purposes," says Tewes. "Now less than one-half of one percent of ocelot habitat remains."

## Setting Aside Land

Because 97 percent of Texas land is privately owned, the hope for ocelots—apart from the 90,000-acre LANWR—lies with landowners.

In a promising trend, says Tewes' boss, Fred C. Bryant, director of the Caesar Kleburg Wildlife Research Institute, some owners are finding that a "wild" ranch can be more profitable than a "tame" one. "Ranchers are discovering they can make $10 an acre on hunting revenues [for deer, Texas doves, ducks and other legal game], while cattle brings about $2 an acre," he explains.

This is good news for ocelots. When Tewes initially started looking for them, his first guides to the cat's whereabouts were friendly ranchers like Corbett and Frank Yturria. "It's ranchers like these who are the future of cat recovery in Texas," says Tewes.

"As controversial as it now may seem," says Corbett, whose 4,500-acre ranch is the habitat of choice for one key ocelot population, "it's the hunters who've saved the ocelot. Our ranch is devoted to wildlife. Thank heavens we didn't clear it all, back when we only farmed and ran cattle." Corbett's ranch is in the federal Conservation Reserve Program (CRP), a voluntary, farmer-government partnership. "The CRP and hunting have saved us. It's too difficult to make a living farming now, and cattle get less profitable."

Tewes trapped his first ocelot on the Corbett Ranch on March 2, 1982. He and his colleagues had set cage traps in promising thickets, but for days failed to bag even an opossum. Then one morning they were greeted at their first trap by a spotted cat, "flagging its long ringed tail at us," says Tewes. "I shouted, 'It's an ocelot!' and promptly crushed my soda can with my bare hands." Thus began the first scientific inquiry into the Texas variety.

## Protecting the Last Ocelots

Yturria is no less concerned with protecting the ocelot. Under a plan worked out with the U.S. Fish and Wildlife Service (FWS) several years ago, he set aside 600 acres of brush in the middle of his 15,000 acres north of the Rio Grande Valley. "I realized I was part of the problem when I found out that the land I was clearing for cattle still held the ocelot," he says. "I'd like to see some semblance of this country just like I remember it as a boy."

When Yturria was growing up in the 1930s, both ocelots and some jaguars made Texas their home. And when his great-grandfather started ranching here around 150 years ago, 6 of the 37 species of wildcats in the world could be found in what is now Texas. Four of them—the mountain lion, the bobcat, the jaguarundi and the ocelot—are thought to remain, though the jaguar and the margay have vanished. (The last known Texas jaguar was shot just outside Kingsville in 1948, and the margay, a sort of miniature ocelot, was last seen 100 years before, near Eagle Pass, on the Mexican border.)

Until recently, ocelots had a reputation as varmints, since they were often accused—sometimes with good reason—of raiding the henhouse. Taking advantage of their taste for poultry, Tewes used live chickens to draw the cats to his traps. That wasn't necessarily bad news for the bait. The chickens were safe in separate cages at the rear of the traps and even viewed captured ocelots as a food source. "I often found them picking ticks off an ocelot's head in the trap," says Tewes.

Ocelots in the wild will go after rodents, rabbits, birds, snakes, lizards and even fish. Some naturalists say they'll also stalk bigger game—red brocket deer and squirrel monkeys.

Noted Smithsonian mammalogist Louise Emmons, in her classic 1980s study of ocelots in Peru, reports they seem fond of playing with their food: "Once in Peru I watched an ocelot walk out on the path with a baby Proechimys [spiny rat] in its mouth. . . . It put it down and let it run away briefly before pouncing on it. It repeated its 'game' several times, alternately batting the baby rat a bit with its paw—just as we've all seen domestic cats do—before finally picking it up in its mouth and heading back into the forest . . . presumably to nosh on its catch."

In contrast to our stereotypical view of the cat as a loner, Emmons' work suggests that ocelots may have a more social lifestyle than fellow felines such as jaguars, pumas and tigers. "Although the sexes each maintained individual territories and, as is usual among many cat species, a dominant male's territory overlapped several female tracts," she recounted, "the cats would often meet and spend time together. And this included at least two males, a father and son, who, one would expect, wouldn't have tolerated each other."

One of Tewes' Texas colleagues, Linda Laack, 41, an FWS field biologist at LANWR, reports that ocelots are "solitary but hardly antisocial." Ocelot mothers, she says, are dutiful. "Usually, they protect the kittens by moving them from den to den, sometimes as often as five times in their first few months." Dens are located on the ground, well hidden and defended by thorn scrub. Once, though, Laack noted that a mother had stashed her kitten in a tree before going out hunting. "There I was, intent on setting a trap at the base of a tree," she says, "when suddenly it was 'raining' cats. The kitten landed near me before it quickly bounded away." Females teach their young to hunt, and if there is enough food, they will take motherhood one step further by setting their daughters up in a kind of land tenure system. "They'll subdivide their territory to accommodate their daughters," says Laack. "But sons, too, are allowed to hang around for a couple of years, as long as the mother is still associated with the son's father. Or it may be that they stay with mom or in her territory for longer, to further mature and hone survival skills."

## Fighting for Territory

For an ocelot in Texas—with only a few thousand free acres of possible habitat, separated by vast tracts of farms, ranches, development and highways—finding a territory is especially challenging. One young male from the Yturria Ranch managed to cross a 27-mile gantlet of highways, roads and farmland before being hit by a car and killed near Harlingen.

"Vehicles are the enemy," says Tewes. "In the last few years at least 20 ocelots have been killed by them." The Texas Department of Transportation has been experimenting with culvert underpasses for ocelots and other wildlife, and the FWS is continuing its 20-year project to develop a wildlife corridor along the Rio Grande.

"Once an ocelot does get a territory, it takes a lot of the male's time to access females and defend his right to them," says Tewes. A case in point, he says, involved "a macho male that I had tracked for a couple of years at LANWR. Soon M61, as we called him, moved in on a female, F30, who was already part of the harem of the resident male, M35. M61 kicked M35 out of F30's life. When M35 got killed by a car, M61 moved in, grabbing territory right and left and, with a certain bravado, claiming another M35 female as well."

Females, too, have to fight for good-quality range. F88, known as Sabia, is one example. Laack first found her as a 2-week-old kitten in 1985. She soon discovered that the cat didn't hesitate to assert herself, and F88 picked up scars from many battles. First she chased away another female from a sub-territory she inherited from her mother. But she seemed to dream of greener pastures—or perhaps pricklier ones. By February 1988, when she was 2 years old, she had established a home range on the choicest parcel around the Granjeno, a little more than a mile from her birthplace. Here Laack tracked her for ten years, losing her once for five years when her collar dropped off, only to retrap her in 1996, then lose her again in 1998.

At dusk one day, I am alone again in a borrowed pickup truck, patrolling LANWR and hoping for another ocelot sighting. Peccaries play on the road, looking in the fading light like rollicking plush toys. A flock of redhead ducks passes over, and a pair of ospreys leap from one dead yucca to another. Then, high on a hill above the laguna, a good-sized cat strides along the ledge of an overlook used by birdwatchers. A bobcat? Too refined, I think. Although bobcats and ocelots weigh about the same, a bobcat is the tough-guy rugby fan in full bellow, while an ocelot is the reserved spectator at Wimbledon's center court. When darkness falls, I hear a distinct meow.

Back at LANWR headquarters, I keep my own counsel. Who would believe that I spotted another ocelot? A week later, though, Laack e-mails me: "You are going to be so envious. I trapped a new male ocelot!" Sure enough, it turns out she trapped it near the bird-watcher overlook. A few days later she phones: "We got another one—a female!" Subsequent radio tracking confirms that the two cats are staying in the area and are even hanging out together. "Now that," says Laack, "makes me cautiously optimistic about the future of the Texas ocelot."

# THE RETURN OF THE CALIFORNIA CONDOR

Jeffrey P. Cohn

In this selection, science writer Jeffrey P. Cohn describes the remarkable comeback of the California condor. On the brink of extinction in 1987, Cohn writes, the twenty-seven condors remaining in the wild were captured and placed in captive breeding
programs in San Diego and Los Angeles, California. Since then,
he reports, researchers have successfully released several captive-
bred condors back into the wild. However, the condor program
has not been without its difficulties, Cohn reveals. Some scientists believe that the released condors have not been properly
bred to live in the wild, he explains. However, the condor breeding program has been learning from its setbacks and improving,
Cohn asserts. Released condors are now hatching chicks in the
wild, the author reports—a good sign that the breeding program
is a success. Cohn has written for *Americas* and *Bioscience.*

It was three o'clock one cold November morning [in 2002], and Mike
Wallace was trudging up a steep canyon in the Sierra de San Pedro
Martir in the northern part of Mexico's Baja California Peninsula.
Tired and hungry, Wallace carried a California condor known simply
as Number 59 under his arm. To catch that condor in the dark of
night, he had to hike several miles down the canyon through dense
chaparral, climb sixty feet up a tall Jeffrey's pine to where the bird was
roosting, set up a strobe light to distract the condor, and then grab
and lower it to two of his Mexican crew on the ground while dangling
upside down from a tree limb.

Number 59 was one of three captive-hatched California condors released to the wild a few days earlier in the Sierra de San Pedro Martir.
Before the birds could adjust to their new freedom and unfamiliar territory, however, two were attacked in the air by golden eagles, a not uncommon danger for condors. Number 59 retreated to the safety of trees
in the heavily forested mountainside. The few times the frightened bird
ventured out he flapped low through the trees, a very uncondor-like
behavior.

Jeffrey P. Cohn, "Bred to Soar," *Americas*, vol. 56, September 2004, p. 22. Copyright
© 2004 by *Américas*, a bimonthly magazine published by the General Secretariat of the
Organization of American States in English and Spanish. Reproduced by permission.

Today, after the dramatic rescue and successful second release on Baja six months later, Number 59 symbolizes both the achievements and problems of reintroducing endangered California condors to the wild. It also symbolizes the personal commitment of researchers like Wallace to the survival of condors. "I've been working with condors since 1980," says Wallace, a wildlife specialist at the San Diego Zoo and leader of the California condor recovery team since 1992. "I never thought I would be doing condors for so long. I have a lot invested in this species."

## Back from the Brink

Once on the brink of extinction, there are now more California condors both in the wild and in captivity in at least a half century. Indeed, captive condors are now so numerous they are housed in four separate breeding facilities in the United States. Some of their offspring fly free at four release sites in two U.S. states and one in Mexico. Reintroduced condors have even begun to breed and find food on their own in the wild.

Despite these successes, the effort to save California condors continues to have problems, evoke criticisms, and generate controversy. Captive-hatched condors released to the wild have died at what to some people are alarmingly high rates. Others have had to be recaptured after they acted foolishly or became ill. As a result, the scientists, zookeepers, and conservationists who are concerned about condors have bickered among themselves over the best ways to rear and release the birds.

At first glance, why anyone would want to save California condors is not entirely clear. Unlike the closely related Andean condors with their white neck fluff or king vultures with brilliant black-and-white coloring, California condors are not much to see. Their dull black color—even when contrasted with white underwings—featherless head and neck, oversized feet, and blunt talons are hardly signs of beauty or strength. Nor have the condors' carrion-eating habits endeared them to many people.

Their appeal begins to become evident when they take flight. With nine-and-a-half-foot wingspans and weights up to twenty-eight pounds, California condors are North America's largest fully flighted birds. In the Americas, only Andean condors are bigger. California condors can soar almost effortlessly for hours, often covering hundreds of miles a day. Only occasionally do they need to flap their wings to take off, change direction, or find a band of warm air known as a thermal to carry them higher.

In prehistoric times, California condors ranged from southern British Columbia in Canada to northern Baja and east across the southern United States to Florida and New York. By the time Europeans arrived, condors were limited to the mountains along the Pacific coast. Perhaps a hundred or more remained by the 1940s, all confined to a U-shaped region in the mountains and foothills north of Los Angeles. By the early 1980s, they numbered only twenty-one.

No one knows for sure why California condors almost disappeared. Probably never numerous anywhere, condors may have begun declining when large Ice Age mammals like mammoths and giant ground sloths, on whose carcasses they once fed, became extinct. Early European explorers and settlers, however, reported often seeing eighty or more condors gathered at a carcass, a sign of a healthy population. More recently, condors were sometimes shot by hunters or poisoned by ranchers who mistakenly thought they killed livestock. Condors also died after eating deer and other animals killed by hunters who had used lead bullets or shot. Ingested lead, a problem that went unrecognized until the mid-1980s, can kill condors and other birds if untreated.

Whatever the reasons, the U.S. Fish and Wildlife Service [FWS], along with several private groups, launched a major effort to study and save the birds in the early 1980s. The effort was based on earlier research and land-acquisition programs. In addition to monitoring condors in the wild, captive-breeding programs were started at the San Diego Wild Animal Park and the Los Angeles Zoo with eggs and chicks taken from their nests. When six of the last fifteen wild condors died or disappeared in 1984–85, FWS officials decided to capture the remaining birds. In 1987, with the population numbering twenty-seven, the last wild California condor was brought into captivity.

## Increasing the Population

From the beginning, scientists and zookeepers sought to increase condor numbers quickly to preserve as much of the species' genetic diversity as possible. From studying wild condors, they already knew that if a pair lost an egg, the birds would often produce another. So, the first and sometimes second eggs laid by each female in captivity were removed, artificially incubated, and the chicks raised using handheld puppets made to look like adult condors.

Such techniques worked. Beginning with the first chick conceived and hatched in captivity in 1988, 314 California condors have been hatched at the San Diego and Los Angeles zoos and, later, the World Center for Birds of Prey in Boise, Idaho. More than 90 percent survived. The total condor population now numbers 247. That includes 148 birds in the three breeding centers and a new one opened by the Oregon Zoo in Portland in 2003.

As captive numbers rose and worries about the species' survival diminished, the scientists and zookeepers began releasing condors to the wild, at first female Andeans to test methods in 1988 and then California condors in 1992. With the Andeans recaptured, the first releases took place in Los Padres National Forest in Southern California, northwest of Los Angeles. Later, birds were released in the Ventana

Wilderness Area further north in California, along the Vermillion Cliffs just north of the Grand Canyon in Arizona, and in Baja. The most recent release occurred in Pinnacles National Monument in California [in] January [2004]. In all, 174 California condors have been released since 1992, of which 97 remain in the wild today.

From the outset, however, problems arose. The released condors engaged in some reckless and even dangerous behaviors. Some landed on people's houses and garages, walked across roads and airport runways, sauntered into park visitor centers and fast food restaurants, and took food offered by picnickers and fishermen. None are known to have died by doing so, though. More seriously, one condor died from drinking what was probably antifreeze. Others died in collisions with overhead electrical transmission wires, drowned in natural pools of water, or were killed by golden eagles and coyotes. Still others were shot by hunters and killed or made seriously ill from lead poisoning. Some just plain disappeared.

Most recently, in 2002 and 2003, some of the first chicks hatched in the wild—in itself a major milestone for the condor program—died after their parents fed them bottle caps, glass shards, pieces of plastic, and other man-made objects that fatally perforated or blocked their intestines. These deaths may be due to the chicks' parents mistaking man-made objects for bone chips eaten for their calcium content. "We may have to feed them bone chips ourselves," Wallace says, "in order to encourage them away from the man-made material."

## Problems in the Wild

Those losses have led some former participants in the California condor recovery project to question how the birds are raised and released to the wild. "I'm concerned that we have not created a self-sustaining operation," says David Clendenen, a former condor field biologist who now manages the Wind Wolves Preserve in California.

"Mortality rates are too high," adds Vicky Meretsky, associate professor of conservation biology at Indiana University in Bloomington. Meretsky says death rates above 10 percent a year cannot be sustained by a wild condor population alone. The current rate stands at 14–15 percent and earlier reached 20 percent, Wallace says. In fact, more than one-third of all released condors have either died or been returned to captivity, usually within the first two years. "We have an ethical responsibility to fix the problems and not reenact them," Meretsky states.

Clendenen, Meretsky, and others have advocated pulling most if not all released condors out of the wild and replacing them with younger birds that have been hatched and raised by their parents in natural enclosures located in or near the areas where they will be released rather than in urban zoos. The critics argue that puppet-raised condors are too tame and do not know how to be wild condors. "They are caricatures," Clendenen says. The critics also accuse the U.S. Fish and Wildlife Service of doing too little to reduce lead poisoning.

Mike Wallace disagrees. He argues that the condors' problems in the wild have more to do with their immaturity, inexperience and, most importantly, lack of proper socialization. There are only slight differences in behavior and survival rates between puppet- and parent-raised condors in the wild, according to Wallace. Further, because all the birds released to the wild before 1995 were brought back to the zoos, most wild condors are still juveniles or, as Wallace once described them, "goofy teenagers." They engage in more dangerous behaviors than the older birds. Only recently have some condors become mature and started breeding.

Additionally, Wallace says, some of the condors' problems represent natural behaviors that help them survive as carrion eaters. For one, the highly social condors are naturally curious. They watch each other and other scavengers, and follow them to food. In that sense, people are just another food source worth following. Also, the propensity of released California condors to hang around people is not much different from wild Andean condors in South America. Andeans often land near campers and solicit food. Maybe from the air they think the shiny aluminum tops and hubcaps of their vehicles are water.

Further, most captive-hatched birds released to the wild suffer high mortality rates, adds Lloyd Kiff, a former condor recovery team leader who is now science director for the Peregrine Fund. The Peregrine Fund manages the Boise, Idaho, condor-breeding center and the Arizona release site. "A lot of [other] birds are killed when they hit power lines or houses," Kiff says. "A lot of birds hang around people and human structures in hopes of getting food. But no one notices or comments because the birds are not rare."

## Condor Socialization

The real key to successful condor reintroduction, Wallace believes, lies in properly socializing young condors as members of a group that follow and learn from older, preferably adult birds. That, he argues, was missing from earlier condor releases to the wild. Typically, condors hatched in the spring were released to the wild that fall or winter, when they were still less than a year old. Especially in the early releases, the young condors had no adults or even older juveniles to learn from and keep them in their place. Instead, the only other condors they saw in captivity and the wild were ones their own age.

Now, condor chicks at the San Diego and Los Angeles zoos are raised in cavelike nest boxes. The chicks can see older condors in a large flight pen outside their box but cannot interact with them until they are about five months old. Then, the chicks are gradually released into the pen and the company of the social group. The group includes adult and older juvenile condors that act as mentors for younger ones.

"Adults provide leadership and direction on a basic social level," Wallace says. "We want chicks to want to be part of the group, not buddies with similar aged chicks that do not know anything."

In the presence of older birds, the younger condors tend to be shy and submissive. As they get older and move up the social scale, they learn to be more cautious in their actions for fear of being attacked by the adults, says Michael Clark, the Los Angeles Zoo's condor keeper and co-author with Wallace on the new puppet-rearing technique. And more tentative chicks are less likely to get into trouble when released to the wild.

That brings us to Sierra de San Pedro Martir. At more than ten thousand feet elevation, it is the Baja Peninsula's tallest peak. The mountain's higher elevations where the condors were released feature tall pines, spruces, and hemlocks as well as manzanita, a low-growing shrub with smooth, red bark. The ground is littered with large granite boulders. A fifteen-mile-long ridge overlooks deep canyons with ledges for nesting that double as condor launch pads for takeoff.

The lower elevations are dotted with yuccas, agaves, pitahaya cacti, and other Sonoran Desert plants. Ranches farther down the mountain have plenty of dead livestock for condors to eat. And there are few people or buildings in the area for condors to visit. Scientists have studied Baja as a possible release site since the 1970s. "We would like to get condors back in as much of their former range as possible," Wallace says. "This is the southernmost part of their range. It was time."

More than just time, releasing California condors in the fifteen-thousand-acre Sierra de San Pedro Martir National Park is seen by some conservationists as key to preserving northern Baja's natural environment. "The condors make this park more attractive," says Horacio de la Cueva, a wildlife biologist at the Center for Scientific Investigation and Education (CICESE) in Ensenada. "This is an under-explored area of Baja. The condors will be a focal point for scientific studies. They are a spectacular bird that people want to see and be associated with."

## International Cooperation

Beyond Baja, the condors have an international importance as well. "Mexico has provided wolves, black bears, and jaguarundis to help restore endangered species in the United States," says Ezequiel Ezcurra, president of Mexico's National Institute of Ecology. "Now we are the recipients of an endangered species from the United States. Both countries need to cooperate to bring the condor back."

For Wallace, the release of California condors in Baja—five in the spring of 2003 and another six in the fall—was an experiment designed to test his theories. The original shipment of condors included a sixth bird not intended for release—Xewe, a then eight-year-old female. Her presence and calming personality provides a role model for the younger condors, even when they are outside the release pen and she is inside. Also, the released birds were older than most previously released condors, all having spent two years with socializing groups in the San Diego and Los Angeles zoos.

Nevertheless, the experiment might have ended before it had gotten under way. A fire broke out in the mountain's lower elevations that July, just two months after the first group of condors was rereleased. Wallace suspects it was set deliberately "to get rid of us." The fire raced up the mountain, getting within "a stone or two's throw," he says, of the condor holding pen and the monitoring team's campsite. Wallace and his staff moved the birds and equipment to safer ground, bulldozed firebreaks, and put out fires that jumped the breaks. Finally, after nearly two weeks battling the blaze, rains helped project and park staff, Mexican soldiers, and volunteers from Mexico's world-class National Observatory farther up the mountain beat the fire back. The only injury: One observatory staffer, obviously more experienced in dealing with stars than live birds, got bit on the hand while holding one of the condors during the frenzied evacuation.

Unfortunately, fire has not been the Baja condor project's only problem. Sluggish economies in the United States and Mexico have limited the ability of government agencies, supporting institutions, and private donors to fund the project properly. Two of the four Mexican field biologists whom Wallace hired to monitor the birds left when they were not paid. Wallace has also had to deal with suspicious Mexican ranchers and campesinos who aren't quite sure what the biologists are doing.

## Signs of Success

So far, though, Baja's released condors seem oblivious to such problems. The condors, even Number 59, have learned not only to stay away from golden eagles' nests, but also to dominate the smaller birds. They have avoided people as they explore the Sierra de San Pedro Martir and surrounding mountains. And they have followed eagles, turkey vultures, and other scavengers to food.

Elsewhere, released condors in California and Arizona are making longer and longer flights, sometimes staying away for weeks and months at a time. The Ventana and Los Padres National Forest condors have traveled more than a hundred miles back and forth between their release sites. One Arizona condor flew more than three hundred miles north following the Colorado and Green rivers to Flaming Gorge National Recreation Area in southwestern Wyoming before returning. Other Arizona condors routinely fly to nearby Utah and back.

Moreover, both California and Arizona condors are finding and eating food on their own. Dead deer, elk, coyotes, beaver, and livestock make up most of their diet. The older condors in Arizona now find 15–20 percent of their food on their own, says William Heinrich, the Peregrine Fund's species restoration manager, although biologists still place carcasses at feeding sites to try to ensure the birds get at least some lead-free food.

Even more important, the released condors may be on the verge of becoming a self-sustaining population in the wild. One chick successfully fledged in Arizona in 2003, the first in the wild in two decades. Five more chicks hatched in the wild in 2004, three in California and two in Arizona. One came from an egg laid by AC-9, one of the last condors captured from the wild in the 1980s and since released to her old haunts in California. Additional releases [in] fall [2004] will bring the wild populations to more than one hundred, another milestone. Most significant, few wild condors have had to be recaptured since 2001, and more has died since . . . October [2003].

## Educating the Public

Finally, the U.S. Fish and Wildlife Service is working with hunting and shooting groups to educate hunters on how to keep condors and other wildlife free from lead poisoning. The multi-year effort, scheduled to begin with [the fall 2004] hunting season, will use magazine, newspaper, and newsletter articles; educational brochures; and package inserts that accompany hunting permits to encourage hunters to use nonlead bullets and shot.

For hunters who still use lead, the campaign will encourage them to find and clean any deer or other animals they shoot, including hiding gut piles so condors do not see them. "We need to make hunters part of the solution rather than having them feel they are being imposed upon," says Robert Byrne, wildlife program coordinator for the Wildlife Management Institute in Washington, D.C.

For Mike Wallace, such efforts signal hope that the California condor might soon reach the recovery program's goals of 150 birds in each of the two release areas (California/Baja and Arizona) and another 150 in captivity. "We've brought the condor from the brink of extinction and are gradually approaching a self-sustaining population in the wild," he says. "If we can continue to reduce annual mortality to a reasonable rate and improve condor behavior in our released birds, we will have something we all can be proud of . . . a fully recovered species. I believe we're on the right track."

# Rescuing Endangered Plants in the Laboratory

Susan Milius

Susan Milius writes about the life sciences for *Science News* magazine. In the following selection, she reports on how scientists are trying to save endangered plant species by attempting to breed the plants in the lab. Fortunately, Milius explains, plants can often be regenerated from just a bit of tissue from a leaf or root. This means that scientists can take a sample—or even just a seed—from a plant from the wild and use it to create more specimens. However, Milius reveals that the procedure is far from simple. Scientists must experiment with a variety of methods before they find one that works, the author writes, and they are not always successful. Nevertheless, Milius reports that scientists are managing to propagate some new specimens, and they are continually working on ways to improve their techniques, which suggests that hope remains for the world's endangered plants.

There's a rescue helicopter, but it doesn't actually land on the roof of the hospital for the world's most endangered plants. Rather, the tissue culture lab at the National Tropical Botanical Garden on Kauai sits in a trim red bungalow with a peaked roof primarily suitable for butterfly landings. There's still life-or-death drama in the business of botanists working to save the rarest of the rare plants. For example, only one individual plant of *Cyanea kuhihewa*, a gray stem topped by a tuft of straplike leaves, remains in the wild. In May [2003], a select crew traveled by helicopter to the north side of the island of Kauai to visit the plant for a few days.

Waiting in the lab for the helicopter's return was Susan Murch, a biologist who commutes from Toronto, Ontario. She'd come to the lab at 7 a.m. to make sure she was ready when the crew arrived from the airport 15 minutes away. She was awaiting precious cargo: She had asked that the crew members, right before they started home, (gasp) pick a Cyanea leaf.

Susan Milius, "Emergency Gardening," *Science News*, vol. 164, August 9, 2003. Copyright © 2003 by Science Service. Reproduced by permission of *Science News*, the weekly news magazine of science.

## Plant Doctoring

Murch works as a fertility doctor for plants, and she does much the same thing that other fertility specialists do. She brings the latest in hormone chemistry and cell physiology to the aid of faltering reproduction. She deals with extreme cases and has tended to endangered plants in Egypt and Costa Rica, as well as in North America.

This Cyanea needs her badly. The botanic garden grows a few of the plants, but they're all offspring of the same parent. That's hardly an ample genetic foundation on which to rebuild a whole species. Even the genetic variation of one more plant, that loner in the wilderness, would help.

[In 2002], the wild Cyanea bloomed, and the botanic garden spent $1,500 to send a helicopter with pollen from a garden plant for the flower. Like so many desperate fertilization attempts, though, this one failed, and the wild plant didn't set seeds.

[In 2003], Murch has been shuffling between Toronto and Kauai as she sets up the lab to help the island's rarest plants have seedlings of their own. When the Cyanea rescue team arrived with a zip-sealed plastic bag holding a wet paper towel and one leaf, Murch started disinfecting the leaf and snipping it into bits that she may someday be able to coax into whole new plants.

In the world of mammals, high-tech reproductive successes have made front-page news. Yet when Murch succeeds at creating offspring for species hundreds of times more rare than the recently cloned gaur or mouflon, it's months or maybe a year before even readers of *In Vitro Cellular* and *Developmental Biology* see how it all turned out.

The projects may be unsung and chronically underfunded, but Murch argues that for the most depressing cases of impending plant extinction, these technologies offer real hope.

## Small Beginnings

Murch explains that, yes, she really is trying to make new plants from a leaf instead of a seed. This approach can work because plant cells are totipotent, meaning that if they are given the right cues, they can grow into an entire new plant.

The effort to find those cues and regenerate whole plants from bits of tissue dates back to the first years of the 20th century. Scientists found that some snippets of leaves and other plant parts maintained in the laboratory could change into unspecialized plant cells. Then researchers demonstrated they could make such blobs of tissue grow into either roots or shoots depending on the ratio of two critical plant hormones, auxins and cytokinins. Later, a pair of research teams demonstrated that providing the right regulatory chemicals to undifferentiated carrot cells could make them start forming an embryo. Once scientists have an embryo, they can coax it into an adult plant.

Today's tissue culture specialists continue to search for the right ratio of the right hormones to trigger development of more and more species. Much effort also goes into maintaining sterile conditions and coming up with the best blend of nutrients to feed particular plants. For example, Murch often adds regular grocery-store sugar, since the first nubbins of tissue that she nurtures may not be up to photosynthesizing efficiently for themselves. B vitamins often go into the mix, too, because many plants normally rely on soil bacteria to supply them.

Since the early days with blobs of carrot tissue, commercial growers of food and ornamental plants have come a long way with these techniques. Lab researchers found tissue culture expands the possibility of studying corn, soybeans, and other crops. Growers have also explored the techniques. Commercial strawberries and potatoes are propagated this way, as are geraniums and African violets.

## On the Edge

"When I first learned about tissue culture, my very first thought was, 'Why do we still have endangered plant species?'" Murch says. It seemed to her that tissue culture labs should be able to take even the rarest species and create dozens of new plants.

Even though it's turned out to be more complicated than that, Murch remains upbeat, even when she goes to Hawaii. There, the fragile flora evolved without many mammalian or insect predators but has recently been attacked by a multitude of invaders. The state has 292 plants on the federal endangered species list, including 150 species comprising fewer than 50 individuals. And of these, 11 species have fewer than five representatives left on Earth.

Soon after Murch got her lab set up in February [2003], she started with the direst cases, such as the hard-luck shrub called *Kanaloa kahoolawensis*. The last part of its name comes from the Hawaiian island Kaho'olawe, which is 13 miles long and, at its widest, 8 miles across. Goats and other animals introduced by Europeans flourished there, destroying native vegetation, and the U.S. Army and Navy used the island for target practice between 1941 and 1990.

Botanists Ken Wood and Steve Perlman of the National Tropical Botanical Garden were exploring the island in the early 1990s when they discovered two unusual sprawling shrubs on a tall rock just offshore. The shrubs' flowers, in tufts like a mimosa's but the color of cream, bloomed over blunt oval leaves.

Wood and his colleague, taxonomist David Lorence had never seen the plant before, but they consulted a specialist who knew the pollen well. The relatively smooth grains with grooves, typical for a legume, had been turning up in samples of ancient soils all over the islands. Paleontologists had concluded that the mysterious plant releasing this pollen must once have dominated the lowland landscape.

The researchers published the official description of the plant in 1994, declaring it unusual enough not just to be designated as a new species but to have its own new genus. Lorence assigned a generic name that honors the Hawaiian god Kanaloa.

The plants seem to be "mostly male," as Lorence puts it: most of the blooms grow only male parts. But one year, biologists found three seeds from one of the plants. That happy fluke has yielded two shrubs that now sit in a place of honor at the entrance to the botanic garden's rare-plant nursery.

Unfortunately, that burst of luck faded. Horticulturists at the facility have repeatedly failed to propagate the plant by cuttings or grafts. "The greenhouse staff is very excellent," says Murch. Their record glows with innovations in coaxing little-studied species into reproducing, so if they didn't manage, Murch deems the prospects grim.

Waiting for more seeds began to seem unpromising, too. Drought hit Kaho'olawe so hard that in 2001, island managers sent helicopter expeditions out to water the plants. "The helicopter puts one skid down on a boulder about half the size of your desk and you get out—carefully," recalls island restoration manager Paul Higashino. Then the helicopter went back to pick up 400 pounds of 5-gallon water containers. Keeping an eye out for unexploded ordnance on the rocky slope, the emergency-watering crew directed the container drop.

Even with three waterings, one of the plants withered to what a casual observer, or less of a diehard optimist than Higashino, might call dead. "I don't want to say that on my watch one died," he says.

## A Different Approach

When Murch arrived in Kauai, she approached the problem by observing the two Kanaloa plants growing near her lab's front door. From these—by then, two-thirds of the world's K. kahoolawensis population—Murch noted details of the leaf-bud structure and other clues to what sort of hormones and nutrients might work. Unfortunately, there were parts of the plants that she couldn't study, such as the root system.

"One of the challenges of working on the last few [plants] is that you can't destroy anything," she says.

She quickly decided that the petioles, the little stems that connect a leaf blade to a twig, looked most promising as a source of unspecialized tissue. However, Murch counted four fungal diseases and three bacterial ailments afflicting the plants, not to mention infestation by an abundance of insects. The last remnants of a species often are sickly, she says.

Murch gave some plucked leaf-stem samples a big wallop of antibiotics and then spent 3 weeks weaning the plant bits from the drugs by reducing the dosage a little every 48 hours. Only then did she expose the tissue to cocktails of hormones and nutrients. A round of tests generally takes 7 to 10 days, after which Murch works out another set of cocktails and tries again. "You just have to work through the possibilities," she says.

The Kanaloa bits didn't do much for several rounds of testing, but finally, embryo tissue started to form. What did the trick was a mild auxin mixed with a strong cytokinin, one used commercially for defoliating cotton plants to ease harvesting.

When she saw her success, did she whoop and hug people? "No!" she says. "You don't get excited until you can do it again."

The youngsters aren't out of the climate-controlled growth chamber yet, but the planet now has a new generation of 20 Kanaloa seedlings about an inch tall. . . . Murch is working on repeating the experiment.

## Global Colleagues

Among tissue culture specialists, scientists who specialize in discovering the requirements of rare species don't reach anywhere near the numbers of what Murch calls "the corn-and-soybean crowd." Yet the rare-plant specialists have figured out how to grow dozens of rare plants.

The Lyon Arboretum in Honolulu has had at least limited success in figuring out how to culture some 300 rare species, says Nellie Sugii. One of her more dramatic projects began with a batch of little green fruits—they looked a bit like grapes, she says—on a stem delivered by Ken Wood in 1998. He'd visited one of the last half-dozen known members of *Tetraplasandra flynii*, a tropical tree species, and found half-ripe fruit.

Sugii extracted the embryos and nurtured the botanical equivalents of premature babies. After 6 months, with the embryos turning brown, "I was worried," she says. She couldn't bear to throw them away though, and suddenly they began to grow. "Now, in the lab, you can't throw anything away," she says.

The Royal Botanic Gardens, Kew in England also hosts a sweeping effort to propagate rare, fragile, or cantankerous species from around the world. They've been particularly successful with sterile-tissue-culture propagation of arid-zone succulent plants, such as cacti, which tend to rot when disturbed.

Some 30 rare North American plants are now under study by tissue-culture specialists at the Cincinnati Zoo. Endangered species of pawpaw trees in Florida, for example, grow what botanists call recalcitrant seeds, which don't survive drying and freezing in seed banks. "We started with the four-petaled pawpaw—the shoots looked really good, but we couldn't get roots for a long time," says Valerie Pence. She and her colleagues there have now succeeded in culturing three of these pawpaws, she reported in June [2003] at the Portland, Ore., meeting of the Society for In Vitro Biology. Her colleague Bernadette Plair also reported a way around the seed-bank problem. For the dwarf pawpaw, the researchers can now pack shoot buds inside gelatin beads, freeze them, and then thaw the plant tissue for culture.

## Producing New Plants

Praveen Saxena, who presides over a test-tube garden of plant tissue from around the world, points out another plant dilemma that culturing techniques might solve. Saxena, a plant physiologist at the University of Guelph in Ontario, is working with Costa Rican scientists to find a trick for culturing their native *Guaiacum sanctum*. The tree's slow-growing wood is so hard that people have used it to make bowling balls and propeller-shaft bearings for ships. Traditional healers have relied on the plant, and modern medical researchers are now testing its potential against asthma. With so many uses and such slow growth, the population has shrunk sadly. Saxena says that, so far, tissue culture for this tree has proved "very difficult," but he's betting the process will produce new plants more quickly than seeds do. In this species, a tree can take more than 200 years to flower.

In other cases, culturing could save a species from overardent collecting and offer health benefits, too.

Saxena and Murch are finishing a study on the endangered goldenseal, a popular North American medicinal herb. The researchers bought bottles of the herbal preparation and sent them for chemical testing. Some samples turned out to carry dangerously high concentrations of lead, accumulated by the plant's root.

Saxena and Murch have now fine-tuned a procedure for tissue culture of the plant that offers herb suppliers an alternative to ravaging the last of the wild supplies and, incidentally, keeps the lead out of the product. Fortunately, the researchers' tests show that an ingredient that's purported to be medicinally active remains high in the cultured version.

Murch can list many more uses for the tissue-culture approach. Her main message, she says, is a bracing counterbalance to a lot of reports of the gloomy state of the planet's botanical resources. "It's not a hopeless situation," Murch says.

And although she isn't ready to celebrate yet, the little bits of Cyanea leaf have shoots and are "looking good."

# ORGANIZATIONS TO CONTACT

The editors have compiled the following list of organizations concerned with the issues presented in this book. The descriptions are derived from materials provided by the organizations. All have publications or information available for interested readers. The list was compiled on the date of publication of the present volume; the information provided here may change. Be aware that many organizations take several weeks or longer to respond to inquiries, so allow as much time as possible.

**American Zoo and Aquarium Association (AZA)**
8403 Colesville Rd., Suite 710, Silver Spring, MD 20910-3314
(301) 562-0777 • fax: (301) 562-0888
e-mail: generalinquiry@aza.org • Web site: www.aza.org
AZA represents more than 160 zoos and aquariums in North America. The association provides information on captive breeding of endangered species, conservation education, natural history, and wildlife legislation. AZA publications include the monthly *Communiqué Magazine* and the *Annual Report on Conservations and Science*.

**Competitive Enterprise Institute (CEI)**
1001 Connecticut Ave. NW, Suite 1250, Washington, DC 20036
(202) 331-1010 • fax: (202) 331-0640
e-mail: info@cei.org • Web site: www.cei.org
CEI encourages the use of private incentives and property rights to protect the environment. It advocates removing governmental barriers in order to establish a system in which the private sector would be responsible for the environment. CEI's publications include the newsletter *Monthly Planet* and numerous reports and articles on environmental issues, including *Conservation and the Public Trust Doctrine* and *Virtually Extinct.*

**Conservation International (CI)**
1919 M St. NW, Suite 600, Washington, DC 20036
(800) 406-2306
Web site: www.conservation.org
CI believes that the earth's natural heritage must be maintained if future generations are to thrive spiritually, culturally, and economically. CI's mission is to apply innovations in science, economics, policy, and community participation to conserve the earth's living natural heritage, global biodiversity, and to demonstrate that human societies are able to live harmoniously with nature. CI publishes the quarterly newsletter *Conservation Frontlines* and numerous books, papers, and fact sheets.

**Defenders of Wildlife**
1130 Seventeenth St. NW, Washington, DC 20036
(202) 682-9400
e-mail: info@defenders.org • Web site: www.defenders.org
Defenders of Wildlife is dedicated to the protection of all native wild animals and plants in their natural communities. The organization focuses on the accelerating rate of extinction of species and the associated loss of biodiversity and habitat alteration and destruction. The organization publishes the quar-

terly magazine *Defenders* and reports such as *Endangered Ecosystems: A Status Report on America's Vanishing Habitat and Wildlife*.

## Earth Island Institute (EII)
300 Broadway, Suite 28, San Francisco, CA 94133
(415) 788-3666 • fax: (415) 788-7324
Web site: www.earthisland.org

The Earth Island Institute, founded in 1982 by environmentalist David Brower, develops projects to counteract threats to the global environment. EII provides organizational support for programs designed for the conservation, preservation, and restoration of biological and cultural diversity. EII publishes the quarterly magazine *Earth Island Journal*, the online journal *The-Edge*, and the electronic newsletter *IslandWire*, as well as various project newsletters.

## Endangered Species Coalition (ESC)
PO Box 65195, Washington, DC 20035
e-mail: esc@stopextinction.org • Web site: www.stopextinction.org

The ESC is composed of conservation, professional, and animal welfare groups that work to extend the Endangered Species Act and to ensure its enforcement. ESC encourages public activism through grassroots organizations, direct lobbying, and letter-writing and telephone campaigns. Its publications include the quarterly newsmagazine *ESA Today*, the daily news digest *GREENlines*, and books such as *The Endangered Species Act: A Commitment Worth Keeping*, as well as articles, fact sheets, position papers, and bill summaries regarding the Endangered Species Act.

## National Wildlife Federation (NWF)
11100 Wildlife Center Dr., Reston, VA 20190-5362
(800) 822-9919
Web site: www.nwf.org

Founded in 1936, the NWF is the largest wildlife protection organization in the United States. It is dedicated to educating and empowering people about how to protect wildlife and habitat for future generations. NWF sponsors National Wildlife Week and education programs such as NatureLink. The organization has a large library of conservation-related publications, which include *Ranger Rick's Go Wild* and *National Wildlife*. NWF also publishes the monthly e-newsletter *Wildlife Online*.

## The Nature Conservancy
4245 N. Fairfax Dr., Suite 100, Arlington, VA 22203-1606
(800) 628-6860
e-mail: comment@tnc.org • Web site: http://nature.org

The mission of the Nature Conservancy is to preserve the plants, animals, and natural communities that represent the diversity of life on earth by protecting the lands and waters they need to survive. The organization uses nonconfrontational, science-based plans to work with communities, businesses, and individuals to save land. It publishes the quarterly *Nature Conservancy* magazine, the e-newsletter *Great Places*, and numerous scientific studies, papers, reports, and books.

## PERC
2048 Analysis Dr., Suite A, Bozeman, MT 59718
(406) 587-9591 • fax: (406) 586-7555
e-mail: perc@perc.org • Web site: www.perc.org

PERC is a research center that provides solutions to environmental problems based on free-market principles and the importance of property rights. Its activities include research and policy analysis, outreach through conferences and publications, and environmental education. PERC publications include the quarterly newsletter *PERC Report* and papers in the PERC Policy Series dealing with environmental issues.

### Rainforest Alliance
665 Broadway, Suite 500, New York, NY 10012
(888) 693-2784
Web site: www.rainforest-alliance.org

The Rainforest Alliance is dedicated to protecting ecosystems and the people and wildlife that depend on them through transforming land-use practices, business practices, and consumer behavior. The alliance works in fifty-three countries with people whose livelihoods depend on the conservation of natural resources. It publishes the bimonthly newsletter *Canopy* and the e-newsletter *Rainforest Matters*.

### Sierra Club
85 Second St., 2nd Fl., San Francisco, CA 94105
(415) 977-5500 • fax: (415) 977-5799
e-mail: information@sierraclub.org • Web site: www.sierraclub.org

The Sierra Club is a grassroots organization that promotes the protection and conservation of natural resources. It publishes the bimonthly magazine *Sierra*, the monthly Sierra Club activist resource the *Planet*, and the e-newsletter *Sierra Club Newsletter*, in addition to numerous books and fact sheets.

### United Nations Environment Programme–World Conservation Monitoring Centre (UNEP-WCMC)
219 Huntingdon Rd., Cambridge CB3 0DL, United Kingdom
+44 1223 277722 • fax: +44 1223 277136
e-mail: info@unep-wcmc.org • Web site: www.unep-wcmc.org

The UNEP-WCMC was established in 2000 as the world biodiversity information and assessment center of the United Nations Environment Programme. It is dedicated to promoting wiser decision-making and a sustainable future for all life on earth by providing information on conservation and sustainable environmental management. The centre's publications include UNEP-WCMC Biodiversity Series and *WCMC Biodiversity Bulletin*, as well as books, articles, and reports related to current research projects.

### U.S. Fish and Wildlife Service
Office of Public Affairs, 1849 C St. NW, Washington, DC 20240
(800) 344-9453
Web site: www.fws.gov

The U.S. Fish and Wildlife Service is a network of regional offices, national wildlife refuges, research and development centers, national fish hatcheries, and wildlife law enforcement agencies. The service's primary goal is to conserve, protect, and enhance fish and wildlife and their habitats. It publishes an endangered species list as well as fact sheets, pamphlets, and information on the Endangered Species Act.

## World Resources Institute (WRI)

10 G St. NE, Suite 800, Washington, DC 20002
(202) 729-7600 • fax: (202) 729-7610
e-mail: front@wri.org • Web site: www.wri.org

WRI conducts policy research on global resources and environmental conditions. It publishes books, reports, and papers; holds briefings, seminars, and conferences; and provides the print and broadcast media with new perspectives and background materials on environmental issues. The institute's publications include *Fishing for Answers: Making Sense of the Global Fish Crisis* and *Reefs at Risk in the Caribbean.*

## Worldwatch Institute

1776 Massachusetts Ave. NW, Washington, DC 20036-1904
(202) 452-1999 • fax: (202) 296-7365
e-mail: worldwatch@worldwatch.org • Web site: www.worldwatch.org

Worldwatch Institute is a research organization that analyzes and focuses attention on global problems, including environmental concerns such as threats to biodiversity and the relationship between trade and the environment. It compiles the annual *State of the World* anthology and publishes the bimonthly magazine *World Watch* and the Worldwatch Paper Series, which includes "Winged Messengers: The Decline of Birds" and "Nature's Cornucopia: Our Stake in Plant Diversity."

## World Wildlife Fund (WWF)

1250 Twenty-fourth St. NW, Washington, DC 20037
(202) 293-4800
Web site: www.worldwildlife.org

WWF works to save endangered species and to improve the natural environment by protecting natural areas, promoting sustainable use of renewable natural resources, and promoting the efficient use of energy and resources. It is the world's largest privately financed conservation organization. WWF publishes an endangered species list, the bimonthly newsletter *Focus*, and a variety of books on environmental and conservation issues.

# BIBLIOGRAPHY

## Books

Walton Beacham and Kirk H. Beetz, eds.
*Beacham's Guide to International Endangered Species.* Osprey, FL: Beacham, 2001.

Walton Beacham, Frank V. Castronova, and Suzanne Sessine, eds.
*Beacham's Guide to the Endangered Species of North America.* Detroit: Gale, 2001.

Karen Beazley and Robert Boardman, eds.
*Politics of the Wild: Canada and Endangered Species.* Don Mills, ON: Oxford University Press, 2001.

David E. Brown, ed.
*The Wolf in the Southwest: The Making of an Endangered Species.* Silver City, NM: High-Lonesome, 2002.

Bonnie B. Burgess
*Fate of the Wild: The Endangered Species Act and the Future of Biodiversity.* Athens: University of Georgia Press, 2001.

Brian Czech and Paul R. Krausman
*The Endangered Species Act: History, Conservation Biology, and Public Policy.* Baltimore: Johns Hopkins University Press, 2001.

Osha Gray Davidson
*Fire in the Turtle House: The Green Sea Turtle and the Fate of the Ocean.* New York: Public Affairs, 2001.

Richard Ellis
*Empty Ocean: Plundering the World's Marine Life.* Washington, DC: Island, 2003.

Paul Foreman, ed.
*Endangered Species: Issues and Analyses.* Hauppage, NY: Nova Science, 2002.

Bradley Trevor Greive
*Priceless: The Vanishing Beauty of a Fragile Planet.* Kansas City, MO: Andrews McMeel, 2003.

David Liittschwager and Susan Middleton
*Remains of a Rainbow: Rare Plants and Animals of Hawai'i.* Washington, DC: National Geographic, 2001.

Richard Mackay
*The Penguin Atlas of Endangered Species.* New York: Penguin, 2002.

Martin Meredith
*Elephant Destiny: Biography of an Endangered Species in Africa.* New York: Public Affairs, 2003.

David R. Montgomery
*King of Fish: The Thousand-Year Run of Salmon.* Boulder, CO: Westview, 2003.

Stephen J. O'Brien
*Tears of the Cheetah: And Other Tales from the Genetic Frontier.* New York: Thomas Dunne, 2003.

Shannon Petersen
*Acting for Endangered Species: The Statutory Ark.* Lawrence: University Press of Kansas, 2002.

Rosalind Reeve
*Policing International Trade in Endangered Species: The CITES Treaty and Compliance.* London: Royal Institute of International Affairs and Earthscan, 2002.

Jason F. Shogren and John Tschirhart, eds. *Protecting Endangered Species in the United States: Biological Needs, Political Realities, Economic Choices.* New York: Cambridge University Press, 2001.

Stanford Environmental Law Society *The Endangered Species Act.* Palo Alto, CA: Stanford University Press, 2001.

Edward O. Wilson *The Future of Life.* New York: Alfred A. Knopf, 2002.

Lü Zhi *Giant Pandas in the Wild: Saving an Endangered Species.* New York: Aperture, 2002.

## Periodicals

Dan Ashe "A Century of Conservation," *Endangered Species Bulletin,* January/February 2003.

Jeffrey P. Cohn "New Digs for the Ferret?" *Americas,* January/February 2002.

Jeffrey P. Cohn "Steep Slopes of Recovery," *Americas,* July/August 2003.

Ryan Davies "What Does SARA Mean for You? The Species at Risk Act in Action," *Nature Canada,* Spring 2003.

*Economist* "Gorillas in the Midst," November 6, 2004.

*Economist* "Out of the Blue: Trade in Endangered Species," November 2, 2002.

Michael D. Faw "Welcome Back, Big Game: Managing Not-So-Endangered Species," *Smithsonian,* January 2005.

Sasha Gennett "New ESA Amendments: Sound Science or Political Shell Game?" *Bioscience,* December 2004.

Duncan Graham-Rowe and Bob Holmes "Goodbye Cruel World," *New Scientist,* November 20, 2004.

Cendrine Huemer "Natural Evolution," *Nature Canada,* Spring 2005.

Matt Kaplan "Plight of the Condor," *New Scientist,* October 5, 2002.

Deborah Knight "Bearly Making It," *Animals,* Summer 2002.

Kevin Krajick "In Search of the Ivory Gull," *Science,* September 26, 2003.

Margaret Kriz "Showdown at Snake River," *National Journal,* January 8, 2000.

Joshua Kurlantzick "Free-Range Markets," *Foreign Policy,* May/June 2004.

Richard Leakey "Living on the Edge of Extinction," *Ecologist,* November 2004.

Terry McCarthy "Nowhere to Roam," *Time,* August 23, 2004.

Karen McGhee "Saving Gould's Petrel," *Geographical,* September 2003.

Annette McGivney — "Moses or Menace?" *Backpacker*, February 2003.

Eric P. Olsen — "Hawaii Plantsman Confounds Greenies," *Insight on the News*, February 18, 2003.

Fred Pearce — "Why a Dead Rhino Is a Good Rhino," *New Scientist*, October 23, 2004.

Briony Penn — "The Prodigal Butterfly," *Alternatives Journal*, Summer 2004.

Elizabeth Pennisi — "Respect for Things That Flutter, Creep, and Crawl," *Science*, April 2, 2004.

Rob Rainer — "Fighting the Death of Birth," *Nature Canada*, Spring 2005.

Joshua Reichart — "Death in the Pacific," *Ecologist*, May 2004.

Russ Rymer — "Saving the Music Tree," *Smithsonian*, April 2004.

Steven Sanderson — "The Future of Conservation," *Foreign Affairs*, September/October 2002.

Rodger Schlickeisen — "The Endangered Species Act at 30," *Earth Island Journal*, Autumn 2004.

Malcolm G. Scully — "Protecting the Endangered Species Act," *Chronicle of Higher Education*, May 2, 2003.

Daniel R. Simmons and Randy T. Simmons — "The Endangered Species Act Turns 30," *Regulation*, Winter 2003.

Randy T. Simmons — "Nature Undisturbed—The Myth Behind the Endangered Species Act," *PERC Reports*, March 2005.

Nancy Smith — "Saving Rare Breeds," *Mother Earth News*, February/March 2004.

Jennell Talley — "Going, Going, Gone?" *National Parks*, Summer 2004.

Connie Toops — "Raiders of the Last Parks," *National Parks*, Winter 2005.

Katherine Unger — "How Threatened Species May Spiral into Oblivion," *New Scientist*, October 30, 2004.

Craig Van Note — "Victories at CITES," *Earth Island Journal*, Spring 2003.

Geoffrey C. Ward — "India's Western Ghats," *National Geographic*, January 2002.

Timothy Warren — "Conflicts of a Giant Conifer," *Americas*, September/October 2004.

Maia Weinstock — "Endangered Species Act Reconsidered," *Discover*, January 2005.

Kirsten Weir — "Born to Be Wild: Can Zoos Save Endangered Animals from Extinction?" *Current Science*, January 7, 2005.

David Whitman — "The Return of the Grizzly," *Atlantic Monthly*, September 2000.

Todd Wilkinson            "A Grizzly Future," *National Parks*, September/October
                          2002.

Wendy Williams            "Out on Maneuvers: Must Military Training Sacrifice
                          Endangered-Species Protections?" *Animals*, Winter/
                          Spring 2003.

George Wuerthner          "Going Native," *National Parks*, July/August 2001.

# INDEX

Africa Resources Trust (ART), 90
*Against Nature* (documentary), 11
agriculture, ecosystem effects of,
    10–11, 15–16
air pollution, decrease in, 27
Alley Cat Allies, 35
Almack, Jon, 103, 104
Amak Island song sparrow, 50
Anderson, Edgar, 81–82
Annett, Alexander, 46
*Argyranthemum coronopifilium* (plant),
    84–85
Army Corps of Engineers, 30
Arnold, Michael, 82

Babbitt, Bruce, 98
*Babbit v. Sweet Home Chapter of*
    *Communities for a Great Oregon*
    (1995), 46
*Backgrounder* (magazine), 12
Bacon, Francis, 19–20
Bangs, Ed, 106
Bartel, Jim, 96
Baumgartner, Sandy, 102
bears. *See* grizzly bears; spectacled
    bears
beavers, resurgence of, 25–26
Beers, James M., 45
biodiversity, threats to, 16
bison, 32
Bray, Rod, 76
Broad, Steven, 94
Brooks, Martin, 92
Bryant, Fred C., 124
Buettner, Mark, 66
Burgess, Bonnie, 39
Bush, George W., 41
Bush administration, endangered
    species listings and, 51
Byrne, Robert, 134

Cagney, Pat, 69

California condors
    current population of, 129
    need for public education on, 134
    original range of, 128–29
    parasites of, 76–77
    reintroduced, problems with,
        130–31
    socialization of, 131
California gnatcatcher, 96–97
Cambrian extinction, 9
Canada
    cooperation with U.S. in
        endangered species protection,
        106–107
    lack of endangered species
        protection in, 101–102
Carboniferous period, 9
caribou, as transboundary species,
    102–103
Carson, Rachel, 26
Castillo, Carlos, 114
cats
    feral, 29
    hybridization between wildcats
        and, 86
    as threat to native species, 34–35
Center for Biological Diversity, 39, 51
Center for Reproduction of
    Endangered Species (CRES), 75
*Changes in the Land* (Cronon), 24
*Chewing Lice* (Illinois Natural History
    Survey), 77
Cioran, E.M., 17
Clark, William, 32–33
Clark, Michael, 132
*Clarkia* (plant), 84
Clean Air Act (1970), 26
Clean Water Act (1972), 26
Clendenen, David, 130
climate change, potential loss of
    species from, 16
Clinton, Bill, 88